'Something w

Kirsten asked, a
settling over her.

'No. Ready to go?' He forced a smile and his tone was polite—*too* polite. She stopped, looked at him for a moment, a puzzled frown creasing her forehead before she continued on her way.

Joel closed his eyes. He *had* to keep his distance from her. He heard the shower start and forced himself not to think about her standing naked beneath the warm spray, only a few rooms away.

Last night...he'd been unable to control the need to kiss her. He could quite easily become addicted to her...and he didn't really have the time for it. Besides, if he did do something about the attraction between them he'd be prising open all the old wounds that had taken the last three years to heal.

Lucy Clark began writing romance in her early teens and immediately knew she'd found her 'calling' in life. After working as a secretary in a busy teaching hospital, she turned her hand to writing medical romance. She currently lives in South Australia with her husband and two children. Lucy largely credits her writing success to the support of her husband, family and friends.

Recent titles by the same author:

THE SURGEON'S SECRET
THE CONSULTANT'S CONFLICT
A SURGEON'S REPUTATION

THE DOCTOR'S DILEMMA

BY

LUCY CLARK

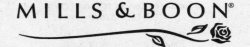

MILLS & BOON®

For Annette—
Without your friendship, I would be a poorer person.
Ps 13:5-6

First published in Great Britain 2001
Harlequin Mills & Boon Limited,
Eton House, 18-24 Paradise Road, Richmond, Surrey TW9 1SR

© Lucy Clark 2001

ISBN 0 263 82708 9

Set in Times Roman 10½ on 11½ pt.
03-1201-51010

Printed and bound in Spain
by Litografía Rosés, S.A., Barcelona

CHAPTER ONE

'WHAT now?' Kirsten groaned as the doorbell chimed twice in quick succession. She continued checking on the cake she was baking before quickly closing the oven door.

Glancing up at the clock, she growled as she saw the time—half past eight. 'If it's another pesky salesman,' she muttered as she rushed through the lounge room to the front door, 'they can go jump in the nearest puddle,' she finished between gritted teeth. On a night like tonight, when the rain hadn't stopped all day long, it wouldn't be hard to find a nice big puddle!

'I'm coming. I'm coming,' she called, slightly irritated with whoever was making her rush. The past few weeks hadn't been at all good and she wasn't feeling very hospitable. The doorbell chimed again as she placed her hand on the handle. 'I'm coming!' she said more loudly, a frown creasing her forehead. Who on earth would be ringing her doorbell on a Sunday evening, in this weather, at this time of night?

She flicked the outside light switch on before swinging the door open, an angry retort on her lips, but she stopped the instant she saw who was on the other side of the door.

'Joel?' Kirsten's annoyance slipped away, in the same way the water was running down Joel's wet face. She heard the taxi drive away as she just stood and stared at him from behind her screen door. His dark brown hair was plastered to his scalp, his long, thick eyelashes were sprinkled with droplets and his piercing blue gaze bored directly into Kirsten. Her heart hammered against her chest in surprise.

Lightning flickered through the sky, outlining him in silver. 'What are you doing here?'

A gust of wind whipped up and blew inside the house. Kirsten shivered.

'May I come in?' he asked impatiently when she made no move to open the door that still separated them.

'Oh, yes.' Kirsten reached for the keys and unlocked the door. 'Of course.' She stepped aside to allow him to enter. He carried two large canvas bags and a walking stick. As he limped through her doorway, she quickly reflected on the conversation they'd had over three weeks ago.

As the faint scent of his aftershave greeted her senses, Kirsten felt a prickle of apprehension wash over her as she recalled that she'd offered Joel a part-time locum position in her private GP practice. It had been the day after the party at his parents' house to celebrate their wedding anniversary. Much had happened since then and she'd completely forgotten about his impending arrival.

Her arm brushed against his as she closed the door behind him. 'Sorry,' she mumbled, trying to ignore the way her arm tingled at the contact. 'Um, if…if you'll wait there for a moment, I'll get you a towel.'

Kirsten hurried up the hallway towards her linen cupboard. She took a deep breath. Joel McElroy, her new locum—her new lodger! Well, almost a lodger. He'd be staying in the cottage that had been built at the rear of Kirsten's house specifically for her parents, but that had been before… Kirsten stopped her train of thought and reached for a towel. She returned and held it out to him, making sure their fingers didn't touch.

'Thanks.'

She watched him unfold the towel and rub his face and hair dry. When he'd finished, he placed the towel on top of one of his bags before removing his thick, winter coat. Kirsten smiled when she saw the way his short hair was standing up on end. 'Where should I hang this?' he asked as he glanced at Kirsten. He faltered for a second before asking, 'Something funny?' He raised his eyebrows questioningly.

Kirsten's smile increased and she shook her head. 'Your hair's just sticking up. It looks…cute.' She shrugged and smiled at him again. This time he returned it. The full force of the gesture caused a flood of tingles to explode within her.

They stared at each other for a fraction of a second longer than was necessary. 'I'm glad I could make you smile,' he said softly. 'From what my sister has told me, things haven't been too good for you lately.'

Kirsten's smile disappeared as she took his coat from him. 'No.' She turned and carried his coat through to the laundry. It still hurt to talk about her cousin's death. After all, it had only been two weeks since the accident. Two weeks since Kirsten's world had been turned upside down.

She remembered now that her good friend Jordanne had asked her permission to tell her brother, Joel, what had happened. Kirsten had agreed but with the funeral preparations, as well as deciding what would be best for Melissa, her cousin's four-year-old daughter, Kirsten wasn't surprised that she'd forgotten some things.

When she returned, Joel had taken off his wet shoes and had walked over to the open fireplace to warm up. Kirsten noticed that the lower half of his jeans were wet, but where he was now standing they'd be dry in no time.

'Something smells good,' he said, his tone bright and cheery.

'The cake!' Kirsten rushed through to the kitchen and hauled the cake tin out of the oven before it burned.

'Looks perfect to me,' said a voice behind her, and Kirsten almost jumped. She hadn't realised he'd followed her. 'What's the occasion?'

She shook her head. 'I like to bake.'

'Well, if you have any leftovers, I'll volunteer,' he said with an enthusiastic nod. 'I'm a lover of great cakes and biscuits.'

'I'm sure you are. I guess it's just as well your mother is a great cook.'

Joel nodded. 'That's *why* I'm a lover of great cakes and biscuits. We always knew when Mum was stressed because she'd be in the kitchen, whipping up a storm. She said that baking relaxed her. It also kept the rest of us out of her way because if we went into the kitchen we were always given a job to do,' he added in a stage whisper.

Kirsten found herself smiling again as she took the cake out of the lined tin. He breathed in deeply and licked his lips. 'Mmm. Smells like Mum's special chocolate cake.'

'It should do. It's her recipe.'

'Really?'

'You forget, Joel, I used to hang around your house a lot, back when Jordanne and I were in med school.'

'Did we ever meet?'

'Yes.' She looked down at the cake, her smile gone. She'd met Jordanne's sister *and* all four of her brothers at one time or another, and although the McElroy men all had similar colouring, there was something about Joel that had stood out in her memory. Perhaps it was the fact that he'd been the jetsetter, the traveller of the family. His skiing competitions had taken him all over the world and when he'd won the silver medal in the Olympics, she'd been at his parents' house, watching the event with the rest of his family.

'When?' He seemed surprised.

She shrugged. 'When I was in my second year at med school. You were back for a few weeks after one of your ski comps.'

He smiled and nodded. 'I always needed to come home

after an intense competition. Just being around family helped so much.'

'Normality?'

'Something like that.' Joel was eyeing the cake appreciatively.

'Would you like a piece?'

'I thought you'd never ask.' He grinned, his eyes alive with expectation.

Kirsten shook her head and chuckled, getting out two plates.

As she cut into the cake he said, 'It always tasted better when it was still warm.'

'Warm cake can give you indigestion.'

'Says who?' he teased as he accepted the plate from her. Not waiting for a cake fork, Joel picked up his piece and took a big bite. 'Mmm,' he groaned moments later and nodded at Kirsten. 'Delicious,' he mumbled with his mouth full.

Kirsten found herself laughing again, and for the first time since the tragedy she took in a very deep breath that didn't hurt. Helping herself to a forkful of cake, she savoured the taste. When she'd swallowed, she looked at him. 'Thank you, Joel.'

'You're welcome,' he said, and she knew immediately that he knew exactly what she was thanking him for. 'If you want to talk about it—any time—feel free to knock on my door. It's difficult when you lose someone you love.' His words had a slight edge to them and it made Kirsten wonder whether *he'd* lost someone close to him.

Tears misted again in Kirsten's eyes and she nodded. 'Tea?' Without waiting for him to answer, she turned away and concentrated on filling the kettle. Her hand was shaking, which caused her to get water all over the place. She sniffed, trying desperately to hold back the mounting tears, but as she felt one slip down her cheek she knew she was fighting a losing battle.

'Here,' he said from behind her. He nudged her aside and took over filling the kettle. Kirsten buried her face in her hands, her shoulders shaking as she once again began to cry.

'Hey,' Joel said softly, and the next thing she knew, his firm arms were around her, holding her protectively against his chest. Kirsten felt the flood she'd been valiantly attempting to hold at bay burst forth from within her and she pressed her face into his warm woollen jumper.

'Let it out,' he murmured as he stroked her long auburn hair, which was flowing loose down her back. 'Let it out.'

Kirsten took him at his word. 'My cousin Jacqui was like a sister to me,' she said between the tears. 'Her own parents died when she was a teenager and she came to live with us. Then, after a few months, my parents filed to adopt her and she became my sister in every sense of the word. We were very close.' The last word was barely audible and Kirsten swallowed. 'Now she's gone and I have the responsibility of her four-year-old daughter. Melissa hasn't spoken since her mother and father died, except for her nightmares every night, and she's hardly eating a thing.' She sniffed. 'What am I going to do?'

Sobs racked Kirsten's body. After a few minutes they began to subside. Joel's kindness had prised open the floodgates and now his kindness was helping to close them. Kirsten sniffed again, suddenly aware of his firm, muscled torso—even beneath the thick jumper. Again his aftershave teased at her senses and she could hear his heart beating. She felt safe.

Joel held her for a minute longer before, reluctantly, Kirsten pulled away.

'I'm sorry,' she whispered.

'Don't apologise.' Joel shook his head for emphasis.

A loud, ear-cracking sound split the air, and even through the closed kitchen curtains they could see the sky light up.

Struck by lightning, Kirsten thought as they looked from the window to each other. That was kind of how she felt—as though her world had been struck and had turned upside down.

She continued to look at Joel, neither willing to break the contact. Kirsten licked her lips and pushed some wisps of hair out of her eyes. She must look a sight, she realised, and was disgusted with herself for breaking down in front of an almost total stranger.

It was true that she had been connected with Joel's family for years but she knew very little about who *he* really was. She knew he could have said the same about her. What Kirsten *did* know was that she'd always been attracted to him—ever since that one time they'd met, all those years ago.

When Jordanne had suggested she ask Joel to help her out in her GP practice, Kirsten had weighed up the pros and cons in a logical manner but one pro, which was by no means logical, had been her attraction to the man.

She guessed it stemmed from both of her good friends, Sally and then Jordanne having found true love in the past few months. It had always been the three of them and now, although they still had their girls' nights out, they were few and far between.

So Kirsten had taken a chance and had asked Joel if he'd like to work part-time in her general practice while he continued his recuperation from a bad knee injury. Little had she known how her world would be turned upside down within such a short space of time. So much so that she'd forgotten all about his arrival date which they'd both agreed on weeks ago.

Right now, though, he was staring into her green eyes and she was staring right back into his blue ones. The hair on top of his head had started to dry, still all tousled and stuck in the air. There was no doubt about it, Joel McElroy was one very handsome man. He was frowning slightly and Kirsten wondered whether he was trying to figure out a nice way of telling her he'd reconsidered. She wouldn't have blamed him in the slightest.

The thought was enough to help her break the spell and she turned and walked out of the kitchen. She was glad when he didn't follow and she quickly pulled some sheets and fresh towels out of the linen cupboard.

When she returned, he'd switched the kettle on and was helping himself to another piece of cake. At least he had a healthy appetite. He gave her a sheepish grin when he saw her.

'I can't help myself. You're delicious.'

Kirsten's eyes widened at his words and her mouth went instantly dry.

'I mean, your *cake* is delicious,' he corrected quickly. '*Cake*. You're a good cook.' He took a big bite as though to prove his point as well as stopping himself from saying anything else.

Kirsten wasn't sure what to say so she hugged the linen close to her chest and cleared her throat. 'I confess, with everything else that's happened in the past few weeks, I'd forgotten you were coming this evening.'

'I figured as much,' he said after he'd swallowed.

'So...um...you'd better sleep in the guest room here tonight. I haven't turned the heating on in the cottage and it *is* rather cold out there.'

Joel watched her intently for a few seconds before shaking his head. 'I'll sleep in the cottage,' he said. 'It'll soon warm up.' He stepped forward and held out his hands for the linen. 'Thanks for the offer, though.'

'But it's cold.'

'Trust me, Kirsten. I've slept in colder places than

Canberra. You forget that I'm at home in below-freezing temperatures. What serious skier isn't?' He took the linen from her.

'Sorry. I forgot. I'm a summer person,' she told him. 'Don't like the cold all that much.' Kirsten knew she was rambling and was almost glad when a loud pounding at her front door interrupted them.

'What *now*?' Kirsten threw her arms out wide as her exasperation increased. She left Joel where he was and hurried to the door. She was frowning as she opened the door but once more it disappeared at the sight of her neighbour, Stephanie Behr, looking like a drowned rat.

'Stephanie?' Kirsten quickly opened the door. 'What's wrong?'

'Quickly. It's Ian.' Stephanie had tears streaming down her face and her voice was almost hysterical. 'He's fallen off the roof.' Stephanie was motioning Kirsten out of her house.

'The roof!' Kirsten couldn't believe it. 'Let me get my bag,' she said. 'Joel!' she called as she dashed into her room and grabbed her medical bag. 'Can you grab the coats and a torch from the laundry, please, and give me a hand?' She headed for the door. 'My neighbour's son has fallen off the roof,' she explained as she checked the contents of her bag whilst tying her hair back. When Joel handed her the bright yellow raincoat, she put it on, tucked her hair inside it to keep it out of the way and drew the hood on.

'Got everything?' he asked.

She nodded. 'Yes.'

'Let's go.'

Stephanie was impatiently urging them on as all three tramped across the sodden grass between Kirsten's and Stephanie's houses. She was glad there were no fences at the front of the property as it would have taken them longer.

'That last lightning strike, hit our house,' Stephanie explained in a rush, her voice shaking. 'Ian was on the roof, fixing the aerial. His friend said he was holding on to the aerial when the lightning struck.'

That didn't sound too good but Kirsten said lightly, 'There must have been a cricket match on television.' She knew how fanatical her sixteen-year-old neighbour was about cricket.

'Yes. I was in my room, reading, and one of his friends who's here came and got me. I had no idea he'd climbed up on the roof.' There was a hint of anger mixed with the worry in Stephanie's tone.

'Can't be helped now,' Kirsten replied.

'There he is.' Stephanie pointed to where they could see a boy lying on the ground, just off to the side of the house in Stephanie's rock garden. He was visible in the beam from a torch one of his friends was holding. The front of the house was lit up like a Christmas tree.

They all hurried over. Another friend appeared from inside, an umbrella over his head. He reached Ian at the same time they did and crouched down, holding the umbrella over Ian's supine form.

'Don't touch him,' Kirsten and Joel said in unison. Kirsten knelt down near Ian's face and pressed her fingers to his carotid pulse. 'Ian?' she called loudly. 'Can you hear me, Ian? It's Kirsten, from next door.' No response. 'Pulse is faint,' she said to Joel, who was kneeling on the other side of the patient. 'Stephanie, call an ambulance. You...' She pointed to the boy holding the torch. 'Can you get some blankets, please? Give your friend the torch.' Without a word, they both rushed off.

Kirsten pulled on her gloves before checking that Ian hadn't swallowed his tongue and that his airway was clear. 'No obstruction. Good.'

'Why can't we take him inside?' the boy holding the umbrella as well as the torch asked.

'He might have a spinal injury,' Kirsten replied as she opened her bag and pulled out a medical torch. Checking Ian's pupils, she reported, 'Reacting to light.' She returned the torch to her bag. Next she set up her portable sphygmomanometer to take Ian's blood pressure. 'BP one hundred and ten over fifty.'

'Keep monitoring for dysrhythmia,' Joel said, and Kirsten nodded.

'What's that?' the boy asked sceptically.

'What's your name?' Kirsten asked him.

'Dwaine. My brother's Damian. What's that dis-rhythm thing?'

'It's common for a person who's been electrocuted, as Ian has, to have an irregular heartbeat,' Kirsten explained quickly before she called Ian's name once more. Still no response.

'Why doesn't he answer?' Dwaine asked, his tone curious as well as worried.

'He's unconscious,' Joel replied, as he pulled on a pair of medical gloves before running his hands over Ian's bones, checking for fractures. 'Right humerus doesn't feel too good and his left hip appears to be dislocated.'

'Can you put it back in?' Dwaine asked again.

'No,' Joel replied. 'It needs to be X-rayed first to ensure there are no fractures to the bone. How are you holding up?' Joel asked, not looking at the boy but continuing to check Ian's legs. 'You're not queasy, are you?'

'No,' Dwaine said through chattering teeth. 'Just cold.'

'When Ian's mum gets back, go inside and put some dry clothes and a coat on,' Joel instructed. 'We don't want to be treating you as well,' he said. 'Left tibia is fractured but the right leg feels fine,' he told Kirsten, who had been preparing everything she would need to set up an IV line.

'IV in left arm?' she asked.

'Yes.'

Kirsten changed sides to allow her better access to Ian's

left arm so she could set up the intravenous line to boost his fluid intake. The rain and wind were cold on her gloved hands but she forced them to work. She cut away Ian's jumper and shirt from his uninjured arm, giving her access to his skin.

'Both hands are badly burnt,' Joel announced. 'It looks as though the current entered in one hand and out the other.' He looked up at Dwaine. 'Did you see what happened?'

'No. I was inside but Damian was out here with Ian. *He's* the queasy one.'

Joel nodded and proceeded to cover the wounds with a dry, sterile dressing from Kirsten's bag.

Stephanie returned, holding the blankets. 'Where do you want these?' she asked, holding an umbrella as well.

'Just drape them over him—gently. And can you put one around Dwaine? He's doing a great job,' Kirsten stated, not looking up from her work. 'Thanks.'

'The ambulance is on its way,' Stephanie reported. 'I've called your father, Dwaine, and he's coming around to get both of you. Damian's lying down because he was feeling faint. How's Ian?' Stephanie's tone was filled with desperation.

Kirsten's gaze flicked briefly to Stephanie before returning to her work. 'I won't lie to you, Steph. It's too soon to say.' Kirsten's tone was sympathetic and she'd have given anything to have been able to put her arms around her neighbour in comfort, but Ian's needs definitely came first. 'He needs oxygen and to be seen by a plastic surgeon for the burns on his hands and an orthopaedic surgeon for his fractures.'

At Kirsten's words, Stephanie broke down into tears. 'I can't lose him. Not so soon after Bruce.'

'We're doing everything we can,' Joel promised. 'Why don't you quickly go and get into some dry clothes so that when the ambulance arrives, you're ready to go?'

'Yes, yes.' Stephanie rushed away.

'How are you holding up, Dwaine?' he asked.

'OK.' Dwaine's teeth were chattering worse than before.

'You're doing a good job. It won't be too much longer now. Who's Bruce?' he asked softly.

'Her husband,' Kirsten answered. 'He died of lung cancer twelve months ago.'

'Any more children?'

'No. She only has Ian now.'

Joel shook his head in sympathy. 'I've almost finished the dressing. How's the IV coming along?'

'It's just started.'

'Checking his vital signs again,' Joel announced as he took the medical torch out of Kirsten's bag.

'We need to assume his spine has been damaged and follow correct procedure for a spinal injury.'

'Pupils still reacting to light.' Joel checked Ian's blood pressure. 'One hundred and ten over fifty-five. Pulse is irregular.' His gaze met Kirsten's over their patient's body.

'He's about to go,' she whispered. 'Where's that oxygen! Ian? Can you hear me, Ian?' she called again, hoping to get through to him.

'What…what's happening?' Dwaine asked.

'Dysrhythmia,' Kirsten said.

'Try and keep the torch still, mate,' Joel said, monitoring Ian closely. 'I know you're cold but you're doing a great job. We still need your help.'

Joel's fingers were pressed firmly to Ian's carotid pulse. Within a few seconds he announced, 'Pulse has stopped. Breathing stopped.' He pinched Ian's nose and clamped his mouth over Ian's, breathing five breaths into the teenager's body.

Kirsten knelt in the position to perform cardiopulmonary resuscitation. She started to count. 'One, one thousand, two, one thousand…' When she reached fifteen compressions, Joel breathed into Ian's mouth again.

A sob sounded from Dwaine's direction but they both had to ignore it. She could hear the wail of the ambulance siren but blocked that out, too. They had to concentrate on the job at hand. Two minutes later, the ambulance pulled up in the driveway.

'Over here,' Dwaine yelled, and the paramedics rushed over. Stephanie came out as well.

'We've got a pulse!' Joel shouted, a mixture of elation and relief in his tone. 'Get that oxygen over here.' Joel fitted the oxygen mask around Ian's mouth and nose as Kirsten sat back on her heels and took a deep breath. She glanced over at Stephanie, who was trembling and sobbing.

'I'll hand over,' Joel said softly to Kirsten. 'You take care of Stephanie. Dwaine, you were brilliant.' Joel patted him on the shoulder before taking the torch and umbrella from him. 'Go and get changed.'

'H-h-he's OK?' Dwaine asked through severely chattering teeth.

'He should be. Get changed,' Joel repeated gently, and urged the teenager to go.

Kirsten stood and stripped off her gloves, placing them in a plastic bag from her medical bag. Crossing to Stephanie's side, she enveloped her neighbour in a hug as Joel and the paramedics organised for Ian to be transferred to a stretcher.

'Is he…?' Stephanie couldn't finish the question.

'He stopped breathing but he's doing fine now, especially with the oxygen.'

'I'm so glad you were home. I didn't know what else to do.'

'You did the right thing. I'm also glad that Joel was here. It would have been a lot harder to handle on my own. Now, are you ready to go?'

'Yes.'

'Good. I'll follow you to the hospital in my car and Joel

will stay and make sure Dwaine and Damian are all right. Give me your keys and I'll get him to lock up for you.'

Stephanie did as she was told and wrung her hands together while she waited for Ian to be lifted into the ambulance.

'I'll see you at the hospital,' Kirsten said to her before Joel shut the back doors of the ambulance.

When mother and son had gone, Kirsten and Joel went inside to sort out Dwaine and Damian. 'I want to take Dwaine with me to the hospital,' Kirsten said quietly. 'Just to be on the safe side. He might have changed into some of Ian's dry clothes but he's still shivering.'

'Agreed,' Joel said with a nod. 'You also need to get changed before heading to the hospital,' he ordered. 'We don't want you suffering from hypothermia or catching a cold either.'

Kirsten dredged up a weary smile. 'Good idea.' She looked into his eyes. 'Thanks for your help. I wouldn't have been able to manage properly without you here.'

'I doubt that,' he returned, 'but you're welcome, just the same. Now, go and get changed. I'll stay with Damian until his father arrives.'

'You should get changed, too.'

'I'm used to this sort of weather, being wet and cold, remember?' He smiled at her and Kirsten felt her heart pound louder. Their gazes held and they stood there for a full ten seconds just looking at each other.

'Get going,' Joel finally said, his voice suddenly husky.

She wiped the drips from her face with her wet hand and nodded. 'Thanks.' As she quickly and carefully walked back to her own place, Kirsten told her heart to settle back into its proper rhythm. If she wasn't careful, she'd be checking herself for dysrhythmia whenever Joel McElroy was around.

CHAPTER TWO

WHEN Kirsten arrived at the hospital, Stephanie was waiting impatiently in Accident and Emergency for news of her son.

'How are you holding up?' Kirsten asked, with Dwaine beside her.

'Not too well. He regained consciousness in the ambulance but only for a few seconds. Once he did, the paramedic man gave him a needle with...morphine, I think he said it was. Tell me what's going on. *Please?*'

'I'll see what I can find out, but first let me find someone to attend to Dwaine,' Kirsten said. She crossed to the clerk's desk and waited for someone to attend to her. There didn't seem to be anyone about so Kirsten left Dwaine with Stephanie before pushing open the swinging doors to A and E and walking into the staff-only area. She stood in the corridor, not sure where to go next.

'Kirsten?' a deep male voice said, and she turned to find Jed McElroy, Joel's brother, walking towards her. 'What brings you here?'

'Hi, Jed. Ian Behr—he's my neighbour—was brought in about fifteen minutes ago. Multiple trauma and electrocution.'

Jed nodded. 'He's in trauma room two. I'm just on my way to check him for an orthopaedic consult. Come with me and we'll find out what's happening.'

'Thanks, but, first, one of the boys who helped at the accident site is here as well. I'd like him to be checked for hypothermia.'

'Sure.' Jed checked the tea-room and found the A and E

registrar there. 'Sorry to interrupt your break,' he said, Kirsten still by his side. 'This is Dr Doyle who has a patient for you out in the waiting area.'

The registrar took a big swallow of her coffee and stood. 'I was just finished anyway.'

'We need to check on a patient in TR 2 so would you mind...?' Jed didn't need to finish. The registrar waved him away.

'Go on,' she said. 'I'll take care of him. What's the patient's name?'

'Dwaine,' Kirsten supplied, and gave the registrar a brief outline of the night's events.

As they walked to trauma room two Jed said, 'It sounds as though you've had a busy evening.'

'Yes. We just managed to get Ian stabilised before the paramedics arrived.'

Jed nodded. 'When did Joel arrive?'

'About ten minutes before Ian was hurt.'

'Good timing on Joel's part, then.' Jed walked into trauma room two and introduced Kirsten to the plastics registrar, the triage sister and the intern who were attending to Ian. Kirsten nodded and smiled politely, glancing at the teenager who was hooked up to the electrocardiograph machine, which was monitoring his heartbeat, as well as the electroencephalograph machine, which was monitoring his brain activity. She took a deep breath and sent up a silent prayer that Ian would pull through. She returned her attention to the plastics registrar, who was giving his opinion on the injuries.

'As both hands indicate entry and exit points, this has resulted in extensive damage to the surrounding nerves and vessels, causing tissue anoxia. We can also assume that as the current passed through his body and his heart stopped beating, several organs may have been affected. The paramedic report said he was resuscitated at the accident site?'

The registrar raised an inquisitive eyebrow in Kirsten's direction.

'That's right. His pulse was faint to begin with but after about five minutes his breathing and pulse stopped. We performed—'

'We?' the plastics registrar asked.

'Dr McElroy and I,' Kirsten added, and watched as everyone turned to look at Jed.

'The *other* Dr McElroy,' he supplied with a smile. 'The one that's not me and not Jordanne.'

'Too many McElroys,' the registrar mumbled.

'Dr *Joel* McElroy has just joined my general practice,' she said by way of explanation. 'He was at my home when my neighbour came across to ask for assistance.' This only earned her a few more raised eyebrows but she ignored them, trying desperately not to blush.

'As I said, we resuscitated Ian who responded spontaneously just as the paramedics arrived.'

'Well, you've both done an excellent job,' said the plastics registrar.

'What's the status on the cardiac registrar?' Jed asked.

'He'll be out of Theatre in ten minutes.'

Jed nodded.

'I've called Mr Taylor, the plastics consultant on call tonight, so he should be here soon to take a look at Ian.' The registrar turned and spoke to the triage sister, Renee Bourne, whom Kirsten had met once or twice at hospital functions. 'Keep him monitored. I need a urine test to check his myoglobin levels and also an arterial blood gas analysis. I need the results urgently—could you let me know when they're in? Over to you, Dr McElroy,' he said to Jed, before leaving the room.

'OK. He needs a spinal-column X-ray to rule out any spinal damage for starters.' Jed turned to Kirsten. 'Did you check for fractures?'

'Joel did.' She nodded. 'It should all be in the paramedic report. Personally, I generally leave orthopaedics to the experts. After all, I seem to be surrounded by them nowadays.'

Jed chuckled and the other staff members in the room frowned.

'Sally Bransford, Jordanne and I were all at med school together,' Kirsten explained as Jed performed his examination.

'That's right,' Renee said. 'So, now that Jed and Sally are engaged and Alex and Jordanne are together, I guess you *are* surrounded by them.'

'Except for Joel,' Jed added.

'Except for Joel,' Kirsten agreed. 'But he does hold a diploma in general surgery,' she added. 'And with his work over the years as doctor for various ski teams, I'll bet he's had to do his fair share of emergency orthopaedics.'

'Yes, he has,' Jed agreed. 'From what I can feel, Joel's report is spot on.' Jed filled in the necessary forms for Ian's X-rays.

'When can his mother come in?'

'Let's see. We've had the ICU consultant in to look at him…' Jed ticked them off on his fingers. 'And the plastics registrar. We're waiting on the cardiac registrar and I've seen him. I think that should do Ian for the time being. Just let me get these tests organised and she can walk with him to Radiology.'

'OK.'

'Why don't you bring her up to date with his progress?' Jed suggested to Kirsten.

'Good idea,' Renee agreed. 'I'll come and get her when he's ready to go to X-Ray.'

'OK.' Before she left Kirsten took another look at Ian, hooked up to all those machines, but knew he was in safe hands.

'Well?' Stephanie jumped out of her chair the moment she saw Kirsten.

'He's stable. He needs to have some tests done and a few X-rays taken, then they'll probably take him to Theatre tonight to have a better look at his hands.'

'Oh, dear,' Stephanie wailed, her tears starting up all over again. 'What tests? What did the doctor say?'

'The plastics registrar usually deals with burn injuries,' Kirsten explained. 'He said there was damage to the nerves and blood vessels in both of Ian's hands and that had caused tissue anoxia, which means that there's an absence of oxygen to that area. He's contacted the consultant on call, Mr Taylor, who should be here soon to give his opinion. Right now, they're waiting for the cardiac registrar to finish in Theatre to come and take a look at Ian.'

'Are they any good, though?'

'From what I've heard, they're the best. The other doctor who helped me tonight—Joel. His brother Jed is the orthopaedic surgeon looking after Ian and he appears very happy with the treatment plan. I trust him.'

Stephanie's lower lip began to wobble again. 'When can I see Ian?'

'When he's ready to go to Radiology, you can spend some time with him.'

'Can I go in? You know, when they take the X-rays?'

'I don't think so, but Ian will need you when he regains consciousness. He's going to need to see his mum's smiling face, reassuring him that everything is going to be fine.'

'But is it?'

'As I said, things are looking a lot better than before. He's under constant supervision and his pulse and blood pressure are a lot healthier than they were back at your place.'

Stephanie clutched at Kirsten's hand and looked into her eyes. 'I saw you pumping his chest and Joel breathing into his mouth. I nearly passed out, you know.' Stephanie's voice was barely audible. 'Ian's my life.'

'I know, but we were aware that he might stop breathing so it wasn't completely unexpected. We were prepared when it happened, just as they're completely prepared here.' Kirsten squeezed Stephanie's hand. 'Thanks to your quick thinking, coming and getting me, Ian was able to receive treatment quickly and effectively.'

'I didn't know what else to do.' Fresh tears began to well in the distraught woman's eyes.

'Steph, you're going to need some support, especially tonight. How about I call your mother so that she can come here to be with you?'

'All…all right.'

'Good. Give me her phone number and I'll organise that for you, along with a strong cup of coffee. How does that sound?'

'OK.'

Kirsten got the coffee before making the call to Stephanie's mother. As she told her the news, she sent up another prayer for Ian. At this stage, if there were no further complications, he should make it.

Dwaine's father came to the hospital to pick him up and, much to Kirsten's relief, it appeared the teenager would be fine.

'He was wonderful,' she told his father.

'Good lad,' his dad said, and ruffled his son's hair. 'He's always said he wants to be a doctor.'

Kirsten smiled. 'Is that why you were asking so many questions?'

Dwaine nodded sheepishly. 'I was worried about Ian, too,' he added.

'Of course. I didn't doubt that for a minute. Anyway, you go home and take care—and stay warm,' she added as they started walking away. As she watched them go,

Kirsten breathed a heavy sigh. 'That's *that* teenager taken care of.'

'Talking to yourself again?' a familiar voice asked, and Kirsten turned to see her friend Sally walking towards her. Sally was dressed in theatre scrubs, her short blonde hair slightly tousled as though she'd ripped off her theatre cap and quickly run her fingers through it. Kirsten smiled. Time had been when Sally Bransford hadn't gone anywhere without looking one hundred per cent immaculate. She'd come a long way in a short time, and they all knew it was because of Jed McElroy.

'Hi. Were you looking for me?'

'Yes. Jed told me you were here so I thought I'd hunt you down. How's your patient?'

'In the hands of the experts now.'

'Actually, I was going to give you a call tomorrow about a bit of work here.'

'Here? At the hospital?'

'Yes. I think Alex may have mentioned it—but two positions have become vacant on the emergency GP roster.'

'Is this the one that has GPs coming in once a month on the emergency roster to keep their skills in emergency procedures up to date?'

'Exactly. Alex has offered one position to Joel and wanted to know if you were still interested. I realised it may not have come at the best time, what with Melissa due to arrive soon, but Alex wanted you and Joel to be offered first refusal.'

'Has Joel refused?' Kirsten was interested to know. After all, he would only be working part-time in her practice and she was mildly curious as to how he would be spending the rest of his time. He'd initially said that he could utilise the equipment at the Institute of Australasian Sport to assist in the recovery of his knee injury and Kirsten had presumed that had been why he'd only wanted part-time work.

'I haven't heard at this stage,' Sally responded, looking curiously at her friend. 'If you were to accept the position you'd be rostered on, and I believe your first session would probably be at the end of next week, but don't quote me on that.'

'I'll think about it. Right now Melissa has to be my first priority but I must say that after tonight's incident, I *am* interested in updating my emergency procedure skills.'

'When does Melissa arrive?'

Kirsten sighed. 'Three more weeks. We want to move all of her own furniture and clothes out of her parents' house and into mine so that when she arrives she has all her own things.'

'Your parents have bought a house here, haven't they?'

'Yes, now that they'll be living permanently in Canberra. The house three doors up from me was for sale so they'll be nice and close. They'd originally built the cottage on my land so that when they came to visit they had somewhere to stay, but with Jacqui's death, and now my guardianship of Melissa, Mum and Dad thought something a bit bigger was appropriate.'

'So Melissa will definitely live with you?'

'I'm her legal guardian and I would love it if she stayed with me.'

'How's she progressing?'

Kirsten shook her head, holding on to her tears. 'Not good. Still hardly eating and hasn't said a word since she learned of her parents' death.'

Sally placed her arms around Kirsten and gave her a quick hug before pulling back. 'I'm here for you if you need me.'

'I know. You and Jordanne are a great support team.'

'Hey, that's what friends are for,' Sally said. 'Also, if your parents need help with the move, let me know. If we're not on call, Jed and I would be happy to help.'

Kirsten sighed and nodded. 'Thanks.'

'Oh, good, Kirsten,' Jed said as he walked over to them and draped his arm protectively around his fiancée's shoulders. 'You haven't left. Joel was just on the phone wanting an update on Ian Behr's situation. I've told him the news but he also wanted you to know that Stephanie's house is locked up and secure.'

'Good. I'm just waiting for her mother to arrive and then I'll be heading home.'

'You look exhausted,' Sally said with a concerned smile.

'I feel it, but you know what they say—no rest for the overworked doctor.'

'Hear, hear,' Jed agreed. He bent and kissed Kirsten's cheek. 'You take care,' he said meaningfully.

'I'll call you tomorrow,' Sally said before she and Jed walked away.

Kirsten went back to Stephanie and gave her the message from Joel. As soon as Ian's grandmother arrived, Kirsten made sure both women had everything they needed before wearily pulling her coat on and walking out to the doctors' car park. The rain was still teeming down. She wouldn't be at all surprised if tonight there was a record rainfall for mid-spring.

Visibility was at a minimum as Kirsten carefully navigated the roads home, and she was thankful when she eventually pulled her old sedan into the garage. She switched off the engine and sat in the car for a few seconds, amazed at how every muscle in her entire body ached. Summoning up the effort, she picked up her coat and bag, opened the door and wearily climbed out.

After locking her car and closing the garage, she unlocked the back door and hung her wet coat up in the laundry.

The house was warm and she guessed that Joel was probably still there. Perhaps he had changed his mind and decided to sleep over after all.

'Joel?' she called, but received no reply. She went into the kitchen only to find it very tidy and deserted—all except for a mug that stood in the middle of the bench. There was no sign of the cake and even the cake tin had disappeared. Surely he hadn't eaten that, too! Kirsten smiled to herself at the thought. She walked over to the bench and saw a note beneath the warm mug of…she smelt it…her favourite night-time tea, with a hint of honey.

The note read, 'Get into bed and have a relaxing cup of tea. See you in the morning.'

It hadn't been signed but Kirsten knew who it was from. She glanced over at the cottage front window which she could see from where she stood. There was one light on so she presumed Joel was over there, giving her some time and space.

She momentarily thought about going over to the cottage to thank him but decided against it and simply did as he'd suggested and took the hot cup of tea into her bedroom. After changing for bed, she pulled back the covers and climbed in.

'Mmm. Thank you, Joel,' she said as her body met the warmth emanating from her electric blanket. She sipped at her tea, closing her eyes between mouthfuls, allowing her body to relax. His sweet gesture had endeared him to her even more. She had to hand it to Jane and John McElroy. Between them they'd raised six wonderful and caring children, and Joel was apparently no exception.

Joel flicked the curtain from the cottage's front window back into place. She was home and he'd seen her pick up the tea and carry it out of the room. Good. In his opinion, Kirsten Doyle deserved a bit of pampering.

Admittedly, he nearly reconsidered accepting the part-time locum position, especially after Jordanne had told him about her cousin's death. Now that he was here, though, he was glad.

Joel made himself a cup of tea and sat down next to the heater. The cottage had taken a while to warm up but now at least the chill was gone. After a few minutes of reflecting on the evening's events, Joel remembered that he still hadn't called his mother. Collecting his mobile phone, he settled back into the chair and pressed the pre-set number for his parents.

'Hi, Mum,' he said.

'I was beginning to worry,' she told him. 'How was your flight? How's Kirsten?'

'Good and she's…well, she's getting there,' he replied truthfully. 'Sorry I'm calling so late but there was an emergency.' He explained to his mother the evening's events.

'I'm glad you were there to help, as I'm sure Kirsten was.'

Joel hesitated for a moment. 'How well do you know her?'

'Why do you ask?'

From his mother's speculating tone, Joel could tell she was rapidly forming a mental picture of him settling down with Kirsten. 'Just because two of your children have recently become engaged, you can get all thoughts of me following suit out of your head. I know I'm the last one in the family to approach matrimony but I didn't come to Canberra with the intention of starting anything up with Kirsten.'

'But she's so pretty, dear,' Jane said.

'Yes, she is. All I'm saying is I didn't move here to start a relationship. *However*, should anything…eventuate between Kirsten and myself, then it would be just that—between Kirsten and myself. Besides, I've got the Olympics to concentrate on.'

'That's what I'm more concerned about, dear. You focus so completely on your goal that sometimes you don't realise the…needs of those around you. I'm not criticising,' she said quickly. 'I'm your mother. I love you unconditionally. But, please, Joel, try not to hurt Kirsten.'

'I won't hurt her, Mum, but remember we're both adults with other things to concentrate on than building a *serious* relationship.'

'But there *is* an attraction between you?'

'Mum!'

'All right. I've said my piece.'

'Yes, you have so *now* will you tell me how well you know her?' Joel asked, a little exasperated.

'I know Kirsten *very* well, dear. It was Sally I didn't know well, but Kirsten was at our house almost every weekend, studying with Jordanne, while they were in med school.'

'Have you met her parents?'

'Oh, yes. Isobelle and Greg Doyle have become good friends. I was actually over there the other day, visiting Isobelle to see how little Melissa was doing.'

'When I was still staying with you?'

'Yes, dear.'

'But you didn't say anything.' Joel was a bit annoyed. Jordanne had briefly mentioned that Kirsten's parents also lived in Sydney but he hadn't realised his mother *knew* them.

'I'm sorry, dear. I didn't know I had to report in.' Jane chuckled. 'I guess I'm just not used to having a child at home.'

'I'm hardly a child, Mum. I'm almost forty-one.'

'I know, dear, but your father and I did so like having you here during your recuperation. Although all of my children have left home, it doesn't stop me worrying about them.'

'I know. Kirsten mentioned tonight that Melissa isn't doing too well.'

'No,' Jane sighed. 'Isobelle is going quietly out of her mind, trying to get the child to eat and sleep, not to mention the fact that Melissa hasn't spoken a word since she learned of her parents' death.'

'Poor kid.' Joel's voice was laced with sympathy.

'Kirsten will have her work cut out when Melissa arrives and, although Isobelle and Greg will only be a few houses down the street, it isn't going to be at all easy. Make sure you help her all you can, Joel.'

'I intend to,' he said with a determination that surprised him. This sudden protective urge he felt towards Kirsten had taken him unawares.

'I'm glad you're there, staying in the cottage, instead of living with Jordanne or Jed.'

'No offence, Mum, but after being at home for a few months I was getting anxious to live by myself again. After all, I've done it for almost twenty years.'

'I know, dear. Listen, love, it's late and I need my beauty sleep. Be good. Love you.'

'Love you, too, Mum,' he replied before hanging up.

As he sat there, sipping his tea, Joel thought more about Kirsten Doyle. She'd said that they'd met previously. His mother had said Kirsten had almost lived at their home while at med school, and that her parents were friends of theirs. Jordanne had been good friends with Kirsten for well over a decade yet Joel couldn't recall a single thing about the woman before he'd noticed her at his parents' wedding anniversary party almost a month ago.

He closed his eyes as he remembered watching her walk into the room, holding a carefully wrapped gift for his parents. She'd hugged and kissed them both so warmly that he'd been curious to find out who she was. She'd been dressed in black trousers and a black beaded jacket, her long hair flowing loose as it had tonight.

Joel had felt a tightening in his gut and had been surprised when later in the evening she'd casually mentioned that she was looking for help in her general practice. At that moment, he recalled, all he'd been able to focus on had been the way her lips had moved, the way her smile had warmed him and the incredible way her perfume had wound its way around his senses.

Tonight, she'd looked completely different, dressed in her old comfortable jeans and jumper, her hair loose but looking as though it hadn't been brushed all day and a look of utter exhaustion on her face. Yet, he realised as his gut tightened again, she'd looked more beautiful tonight than she had all dressed up at the party.

Feeling her body pressed firmly against his own, it had brought feelings of another kind—feelings Joel hadn't planned on having for his sister's friend.

'Olympics,' he said out loud. 'I've *got* to focus.'

'Breathe in…and out. Again.' Kirsten concentrated hard, listening to Gail's breathing while her son Patrick lay in his pram, crying. 'Everything sounds fine,' she told Gail, before crossing to look at Patrick. She shone her torch down his throat as he opened his mouth wide to cry. 'Looks good. Fine set of lungs you have there, darling,' she crooned. She looked in his ears and up his nose but was satisfied with what she saw.

'If you'd like to take him out, Gail, and place him on the examination couch, I'll do the rest of his tests.'

The new mother wearily did as she'd been asked and Kirsten thought back to the report she'd received from the district midwife who'd been visiting Gail regularly since her discharge from hospital. It seemed that motherhood wasn't exactly what Gail had expected. Kirsten checked Patrick over but could find nothing wrong.

'Try giving him a feed,' she suggested to Gail. 'That might calm him down.'

'I've just fed him, but all right—anything to stop the noise.' Within seconds the room was quiet, with only the contented suckling noises from the baby.

'So, how have things been going?' Kirsten asked, hoping that Gail would open up.

'All right, I guess.'

Kirsten nodded. 'Is Patrick settling into a good night-time routine?'

'Ha. That's a joke,' she replied with more lethargy than sarcasm. 'No, but, then, he's only two weeks old.' She kissed the top of her son's head.

'OK. Has the midwife shown you some techniques for getting him to settle?'

'They don't work. I guess he's just a fuss-pot, like me.'

Kirsten smiled encouragingly. 'If you need anything or just want to talk, let me know. For today, however, you're both all finished.' She flicked over a page in her diary. 'I'll call around to see you in two weeks' time, in the afternoon,' she told Gail.

'It's not necessary,' Gail said quickly. 'The midwife comes every day.'

'I know, but it's part of my job to check on new mothers at home.' Kirsten waited until little Patrick had been burped and settled back in his pram before standing and holding the door for Gail. 'I'll see you, then, but call me if you need anything else,' she stressed as Gail wheeled the pram out.

Once Gail had gone, Kirsten shut the door and returned to her desk to dictate a letter to the midwife. With that done, she finished up her work and backed up her files before switching her computer off.

'Friday morning, done!' she said with satisfaction. She crossed to the door and as she opened it she was faced with Joel on the other side, his hand raised to knock. His presence startled her a little.

'Oh, hi.' She smiled up at him shyly and watched as his arm instantly dropped back to his side. Their gazes held for a split second, which had happened every time they'd seen each other during the past week. Joel cleared his throat and it was enough to break the spell he'd woven over her. She breathed in deeply and realised her mistake as his aftershave assailed her senses. Quickly she turned and walked back into her office.

'I...' She cleared her throat. 'I was just coming to find you. Ready for house calls?'

'Ready when you are,' he said in that deep and sexy voice of his that had invaded her dreams every night since his arrival.

Kirsten took another deep breath and exhaled slowly before turning to face him. 'I'll just get my bag and we can get started.' As she checked the contents of her bag, she glanced up at him. 'Are you...free for dinner tonight?'

'Uh—yeah,' he replied a little hesitantly. 'Why?'

'Nothing really. I just thought we might go out for dinner.'

'What—to celebrate the end of our first week together— I mean, *working* together?' he amended quickly.

She smiled, loving the slips he made. 'Yes. How about it?' Kirsten bit her lower lip, waiting for his reply. He was dressed in a navy suit and chambray shirt, his tie loosened but still in place. He was a handsome man, but she'd known that for years!

'Sure,' he answered with a shrug. 'Why not?'

Their gazes held again and Kirsten felt a tingle of excitement flood through her at the prospect of having dinner alone with Joel. The phone rang, breaking the moment, and Kirsten quickly snatched it up.

'Dr Doyle. Oh, hi, Wes,' she said into the receiver. 'How are things going?' She waited. 'Good. Thanks for that and keep me informed. Love you. Bye.'

'So...who's Wes?' he asked casually.

The urge to tease him was just too great to pass up. 'My attorney. We've known each other for...*years*. He's handling the legal side of my cousin's will.'

'Boyfriend?'

Kirsten paused for a moment. 'He's a boy and he's my friend, yes. He's thirty-two, single, good-looking and just waiting for some gorgeous girl to come along and snatch him up.'

'Two years younger than you?'

'Really, Joel,' she said with mock indignation. 'You should know better than to reveal a woman's age.'

He raised his eyebrows in amusement and smiled. 'So, are you thinking of...*applying* to fill the vacancy in your attorney's life?'

'I would,' she said, unable to hide the smile any longer, 'but incest isn't legal in this country.'

'Incest?' he asked before he realised she'd been teasing him. 'I take it Wes is your brother?'

'Yes. The elder of my twin brothers by a whole ten minutes. Luke is married and his wife has recently had their first baby—and he's as gorgeous as his uncle.' Kirsten quickly switched her phone through to the receptionist before gathering up her bag and keys. She walked over to where he stood. 'Ready?'

'As I'll ever be,' he said, as he held the door open for her.

'Thanks,' she said, walking out of her consulting room. They said goodbye to the receptionist, who would ensure the practice was securely locked up, and headed outside into the cold.

Kirsten unlocked her door before climbing inside and leaning over to open the passenger door for Joel. He'd planned on getting a car but as they both lived at the same residence and worked at the same clinic, car-pooling wasn't too much of an inconvenience for the time being.

He opened the passenger door and climbed in, the material pulling tightly around his firm thighs as he sat beside her. He settled his briefcase and suit jacket on the back seat behind them before putting his seat belt on. 'Something wrong?' he asked, and Kirsten realised she was staring.

'Oh. No.' She quickly turned away, completely embarrassed at being caught, and quickly started the car. She wished her hair was loose, instead of pulled back in the long braid down her back. At least that way her hair would be able to hide the blush she could feel covering her face.

Joel McElroy had done a lot for her this past week. The depression she'd experienced since her cousin's death had lifted considerably, thanks to his light humour and uplifting presence. She tried to calm her enthusiasm and impatience for wanting the house calls done and out of the way so they could get on with the rest of the evening.

Kirsten had decided that it would be best if she and Joel did the house calls together so that he could get to know the patients more quickly. She knew that when Melissa arrived she'd be reorganising even further the way the clinic hours were structured, and from her preliminary plan it appeared she'd need to hire another locum to fill in, with both her and Joel working only part-time. After all, until Melissa started school, which wasn't for another four months, Kirsten wanted to be able to spend as much time with her as possible.

'You like this old car, don't you,' he stated, his words interrupting her thoughts.

'Yes.' Kirsten smiled as she pulled out into the early afternoon traffic. 'It holds many memories.'

'Care to share one?'

'Sure.' She thought for a moment before chuckling to herself nostalgically. 'One year, after our end-of-year exams, Jordanne and I were able to persuade Sally to come camping with us.'

'She didn't usually go?'

Kirsten shook her head. 'You must have heard that Sally's father, Norman, tried to bribe Jordanne so that she'd make Sally leave med school?'

'Oh, yes.' He nodded.

'Well, from then on Sally didn't like to socialise with us outside university hours in case her father tried any other tactics. She was very cautious.'

'I'm glad, for her sake, that her father has changed.'

'You and me both.'

'So why did she decide to come with you this time?'

'Her father was overseas for a month, conducting meetings. Her mother had gone with him so Sally decided it was safe to come.' Kirsten smiled to herself. 'I'm glad she did because we had a fantastic time. We drove my old faithful car to a conservation park where Jordanne and I had camped before, but this time we decided on a different location. You know, try something new. Anyway, to cut a long story short, we ended up camping near a river.'

'Uh-huh.' Joel nodded, a smile already forming on his face.

'We weren't right at the edge but the ground was nice and flat.'

'Let me guess—the river rose during the night?'

'Yes.' Kirsten giggled. 'It was Sally who raised the alarm. We managed to get everything out of the tent and up onto dry land, but wading through the water was freezing. When we went to move the tent, it had water swirling around inside and that's when I saw *The Book*.'

'The Book?'

'You know, the anatomy textbook for med school?'

'The five-centimetres-thick one?'

'That's it. It was floating around like a little boat bumping into the side of the tent, its pages slowly soaking with water.'

Joel laughed. 'Whose book was it?'

'Mine. It's still on my shelf at home, and every time I need to look something up in its crinkly, water-stained pages, I remember that camping trip and I always smile. Thank goodness we'd parked the car up on the hill. As the tent was wet, we slept in here that night.' Kirsten patted the dashboard.

'That's a nice memory,' he said, and she turned to glance at him before looking back at the road.

'I've always kept the car serviced and had a gas tank installed instead of using leaded petrol. I think it has quite a few more years left in it.'

'You're probably right,' Joel agreed as Kirsten pulled up outside their first port of call.

From then on, she and Joel focused on one patient after another as the afternoon slowly progressed.

'Last stop coming up,' she announced eventually.

'Doris and Fred Dawson,' Joel read out from the schedule.

'They're a lovely pair. They were both born on the same day eighty years ago, raised six children, have numerous grandchildren and even a few great-grandchildren, and are two of the sweetest people I've ever met. Doris has recently returned home from the rehabilitation hospital after a total hip replacement. She's one of Alex's patients,' Kirsten told him as she drove.

'And Fred?'

'He has asthma, which I like to keep a close eye on. The

district nurse has been coming out every day as spring is definitely the season for asthma sufferers.'

When Kirsten pulled into the driveway of the old brick house, the front yard filled with native evergreen trees, it was almost half past five.

'I love this garden,' she said as she climbed out and walked over to touch the lovely red blooms of the bottle-brush tree. 'These are my favourite. They're so… Australian.' She turned and smiled at him.

Joel felt as though a fist had just slammed into his solar plexus at the vibrancy in her gaze. Her smile was full and radiated happiness as she touched the blooms once more. He shook his head slightly before leaning back against the car to watch her. She was a beautiful woman, he'd known that from the first instant he'd seen her, but during the past week they'd spent together Joel knew that Kirsten Doyle's beauty radiated from deep within her. No amount of make-up or beauty products could produce this type of result.

> You know it's almost Christmas
> With the bottle-brushes bright
> Their red fiery flames
> Bring back feelings of delight.

Joel listened intently as Kirsten continued with the poem.

> The summer days are coming
> Bringing hot Christmas cheer
> For Christmas in Australia
> Is like this, every year.

> The red blooms of the bottle-brush
> Lift my heart and make me say
> I wouldn't celebrate Christmas
> Any other way.

She turned and looked at him, noticing from the small smile on his face, that he'd enjoyed her poem. Slowly the smile faded and the intensity of his gaze became clouded.

The sound of clapping helped Kirsten to look away from Joel and the confusing emotions he'd evoked. Right now, she doubted whether he was attracted to her, yet a few seconds ago she'd felt vitally important to him.

'That was lovely, my dear,' Fred said as he slowly ambled across the lawn to Kirsten's side. He was a tall man with a shock of pure white hair that stood out in every direction, his brown eyes twinkling with amusement. 'It brings happiness to me when I see people appreciating my garden.' He wheezed.

'I'm glad,' she said, and reached up to kiss his cheek. 'You're sounding better today than you did last week.'

'Much better, thank you,' he said, and patted her hand. 'And who's this?' He turned to face Joel who had stood away from the car and was walking towards them.

'This is my new colleague, Joel McElroy.'

'McElroy?' Fred said, and squinted thoughtfully. 'Where have I heard that name before?'

'Most probably at Canberra General,' Joel said as he shook Fred's hand. 'My brother and sister both work there as orthopaedic surgeons.'

'Oh, that's right. The young lassie who came out to see Doris at the rehab hospital last week. Funny name.' He frowned again in concentration.

'Jordanne,' Kirsten supplied.

'That's it.' Fred coughed and smiled. 'The old noodle,' he said as his index finger tapped the side of his head, 'isn't what it used to be.'

'I think we'd better get you inside, Fred,' Kirsten suggested. 'The pollen out here isn't going to do you any good.' She slipped her arm through Fred's and then turned to face Joel. Handing him her keys, she asked, 'Would you mind getting my bag and locking the car, please?'

'Sure,' he said with a single nod of his head.

'I like him,' Fred said softly to her as she helped him up the three small steps to the verandah that ringed the house.

'So do I,' Kirsten whispered back.

CHAPTER THREE

'WELL, hello, there,' Doris said warmly from her comfortable chair. 'Come in, dear, and sit down.'

Kirsten continued to help Fred along and he sighed with relief when he was able to sit down and relax. 'How are you feeling today, Doris?' she asked as Joel knocked once on the door before coming in.

'Ooh, I see you've brought a friend along. Hello, and what's your name?' Doris asked Joel as she held out her hand to him.

'Joel McElroy,' he said, and took her frail hand in both of his. 'I'll be working with Kirsten for a while.'

'Why don't you stay and help her out permanently? She's been very busy lately.'

'Don't go pestering him, Doris,' Kirsten admonished lightly. 'I'll have you know that Joel's first love is skiing.'

Doris looked from Kirsten back to Joel. 'Really? There's not a lot of snow in Australia, even in winter.'

'I usually train overseas but come home whenever I can.'

'Joel's already won a silver medal in the Olympics.'

'Really? How exciting.' Doris now squeezed both of her hands in his, excitement bubbling in her eyes. 'Did you hear that, Fred?'

'Yes, I did, dear,' her husband answered.

'You look familiar,' Doris said.

'His sister Jordanne is one of your orthopaedic surgeons,' Fred told his wife.

'Of course. I can see the family resemblance. Your sister is delightful.'

'She certainly is.'

'Do you have any more siblings?' Doris asked, not making any attempt to remove her hands.

'Ha. Does he ever,' Kirsten mumbled.

Joel's gaze quickly flicked to Kirsten before returning to Doris. His smile was all-encompassing and Kirsten knew that had it been directed at her, she would have melted on the spot. 'I'm the second of six.'

'We have six children.' Doris nodded and patted his hand. 'What are their names?'

'Here we go,' Kirsten teased.

Joel looked at her briefly again, his eyes alive with appreciative humour. It suddenly dawned on her that Joel seemed to love it when she teased him. She'd have to make sure she did it more often.

'My oldest brother is Jed—he's an orthopaedic surgeon at Canberra General as well.'

'He's very good friends with Alex Page,' Kirsten added.

'Then there's myself and in age order it continues with Jasmine, Justin, then Jordanne and finally Jared.'

Doris and Fred both chuckled. 'Dare I ask what your parents' names are?' Doris asked, finally letting go of Joel's hand.

'John and Jane,' he finished.

'Marvellous,' Fred said with a small cough.

'I like it,' Doris agreed. 'Why didn't we think of something like that, dear?' she asked her husband, who simply shook his head. Doris then named all of her children, grandchildren and great-grandchildren with pride. Kirsten smiled at Joel who was intently listening to everything their patient had to say.

'You keep talking to Joel,' Kirsten said as she reached for Doris' wrist. 'I'll start on your check-up.'

'Right you are, dear,' Doris said, and did just as Kirsten had suggested, talking animatedly to Joel about growing up in a house with six children. The only time Doris was silent was when Kirsten was listening to her chest. She continued talking as Kirsten checked the range of movement in the hip and watched Doris walk up and down with the aid of a walking frame.

After having five minutes' rest, Fred went to prepare a pot of tea and some biscuits. 'I know it's almost time for your dinner,' Doris said as she offered Kirsten a biscuit, 'but take one anyway. You could do with a little extra meat on your bones. Don't you think so, Joel?'

Joel looked Kirsten over briefly and she held her breath, waiting for him to reply. What *did* he think of her appearance? Did he think she was too fat? Too skinny? She recalled the way his arms had protectively cradled her last Sunday night and immediately her breathing became shallow. In her opinion, their bodies had fitted together perfectly.

'I think,' he said as he took a biscuit from the plate, 'that it wouldn't matter one jot what Dr Doyle ate. She's constantly on the go, only stopping long enough to draw breath for the next task, whatever that might be. Therefore, biscuit or no biscuit, Kirsten will remain just as Kirsten is. Perfect for herself.'

Kirsten looked at him for a long moment. Was he teasing? What did all of that mean? Doris, on the other hand, seemed to understand perfectly and patted his arm. 'Well said.'

Kirsten decided not to dwell on it, especially as Doris was looking from herself to Joel with increasing delight. Matchmaking was written all over her patient's face and Kirsten quickly turned her attention to Fred.

'It's your turn now,' she told him as he finished drinking his tea. After his check-up, she praised him. 'You're doing a good job of managing your breathing so keep it up. I'll be around next Friday afternoon but come and see me or call me if there's any change.'

'Will the district nurse still be around next week?' Doris asked.

'I'd like her to be, at least until you're a bit more steady on that hip. When do you see the physio next?'

'Next Thursday morning.'

'Good. That means I'll have the report by the time I see you next week. All right.' She gave Joel a nod as she packed up her bag. 'That's it. We'll see you then.'

'You'll be coming again too, won't you Joel?' Doris asked, and Fred groaned.

'She's taken a shine to you, mate.'

'And I'm one hundred per cent flattered,' Joel remarked. 'Yes, if everything goes well and I'm not held up consulting, I should be here next Friday.'

'Good.' Doris stood and used her frame to walk to the door and see them off.

'Hungry?' Joel asked as soon as they were back on the road.

'Starving,' Kirsten confessed.

'It's almost seven o'clock so why don't we head out for dinner now?'

'Good idea. Where would you like to go?'

'You're the resident Canberran. Where would you suggest?'

Kirsten stopped at a red light and looked at him. 'What would you like? Thai? Italian? Chinese? French?'

'French,' he said after a pause.

'I know just the place. Jordanne told me about it and said they have great chocolate fondue.'

'I haven't had that for years.'

Kirsten was able to find a space in a car park not far from the restaurant. When they arrived, with no reservation, Kirsten looked around the almost full restaurant and wondered if they hadn't been a bit too impulsive—after all, it was Friday night. Would they be able to get a table? In the past, she hadn't done anything that hadn't been planned, but she'd come to realise just recently that perhaps that was the reason for the feelings of discontent she'd been experiencing.

Soon she would have Melissa to deal with and the simple task of having dinner with a man would require a lot more planning. Joel spoke to the *maître d'*, asking for a table and agreeing that they hadn't made a reservation but had heard the fondue was the most delicious in the Territory.

'Right this way,' the *maître d'* said, and Kirsten was both pleased and surprised to find themselves being led to a secluded table for two.

After they'd been seated, she looked at him quizzically. 'Do you charm *everyone* you meet?'

A slow smile spread across Joel's mouth. 'Not *everyone*, but most people,' he agreed nonchalantly.

'You're teasing me,' she accused, returning his smile.

'It's my turn.' Their gazes met across the candlelit table and the butterflies in her stomach took flight. She was amazed at how, in such a short space of time, Joel had become very important to her. Perhaps it was simply because they were spending a lot of that time together but there was one thing that Kirsten knew for sure. If she didn't watch herself, she'd be falling in love with him before too long.

The waiter came to deliver the menus and gave his recommendations. Kirsten watched Joel as he spoke to the waiter and was surprised when he started discussing the dishes in French.

'What would you like to have?' he asked her. Kirsten realised belatedly that her mouth was gaping open so she quickly closed it and searched the menu in front of her.

It was all double Dutch as far as she was concerned— she'd been more preoccupied with watching Joel than listening to what the waiter had said. Finally, as both men were waiting for her to answer, she said, 'The chicken. Thank you,' she added as she handed the menu back.

Again both men stared at her, and when she didn't venture anything further the waiter simply nodded. Joel and the waiter conversed once more in French before the waiter disappeared to the kitchen.

'Everything all right?' Joel asked.

'Yes. Why?'

Her eyes were wide with worry—he didn't have the heart to tell her that there had been five different chicken dishes on the menu. 'Nothing,' he said, watching her instantly relax.

During dinner, Joel was the perfect companion. He told her numerous anecdotes about his time on the various ski-teams and how he loved travelling to new places. Kirsten had been overseas for six months after she'd graduated from med school but she'd been working and living in Canada and hadn't had much time for sightseeing.

'I had two weeks where I toured Europe but it was one night here, another night there—that sort of thing.'

'And since then you haven't had the desire to travel again?'

'Not really. My focus has been on getting my practice established. Now, though, I'll have Melissa to look after.'

'Kids can bring so much happiness into a household,' he said wistfully.

'Do you like kids?' Kirsten was surprised. Considering his footloose and fancy-free lifestyle, she just hadn't pictured him staying in one place, surrounded by children.

'Of course I like them, but whether or not I'm ready to have any of my own…' He shrugged. 'I confess that I haven't really thought about it. I've been surrounded by siblings, nieces and nephews all my life. By the time Jared was born I was eight and old enough to change nappies and feed him, as well as keeping an eye on Jordanne and

Justin. Jed, I think, had it worse than me, being the oldest, but the responsibilities were always there. I'm not saying that I didn't like it, just that it's been nice for the past however many years to be responsible only for myself.'

'Weren't you captain of the ski-team for a while?'

'Yes. When I won the silver medal, but being part of a team and having *those* types of responsibilities are different from helping out with small children.'

Kirsten nodded. 'I know what you mean. My brothers, as you know, are two years younger so as a child I didn't have too many responsibilities as far as they were concerned. They always had each other to play with so I didn't have them tagging along with me as I got older. Yet owning and running my private practice has been a real eye-opener.'

'How long have you had the practice?' Joel asked as he sipped his wine.

'Five years. I worked at a few different places after I returned from overseas while I saved enough money to open up my own clinic, but within the past few months...' Kirsten sighed.

'Discontent?'

'Yeah, something like that. I've worked so hard for so long for one thing, and now that it's up and running I don't seem to have that challenge there any more.'

'I know that feeling. Challenge is a great driving force.'

Kirsten swirled the wine around in her own glass and smiled. 'I casually mentioned to Sally and Jordanne that I'm not sure what I should do next. Not much later, I have Alex offering a position on the emergency roster at Canberra General.'

'Do you resent the outcome?'

'Not at all. I guess in some cases it's not what you know but who you know.'

'Yes, but Alex wouldn't have offered you the position if

he didn't think you were one hundred per cent capable of doing the job.'

'I know that and I'm flattered, which is why I've accepted.'

'You have?'

'Yes. I believe I have my first emergency duty at the hospital tomorrow.'

'So do I,' he replied, and touched his glass against hers before sipping once more at the liquid. 'What are you going to do when Melissa arrives?' Joel leaned back in his chair and stretched. Kirsten watched the way his shirt slowly rode up from the waistband of his trousers and immediately had the urge to untuck it completely and slide her hands up his firm torso beneath. When he relaxed, she raised her gaze to meet his.

He was smiling slightly, one eyebrow raised in surprise, showing he knew exactly what she'd been thinking.

Kirsten was shocked that he'd witnessed her appraisal of him and she quickly looked down at the table. 'Um…' She searched her mind for the question he'd just asked her. What was she going to do? Yes, that had been the question. 'Ah… What am I going to do? Yes, well…' She reached out a hand for her wineglass and slowly brought it to her lips. What she *wanted* to do was to reach across the table and press his lips firmly against her own, very out of character for her.

After sipping her wine, she chanced a glance up at him. He was still smiling, waiting expectantly for her answer.

Kirsten lowered her glass and cleared her throat. 'What am I going to do…?' Her voice was stronger now as she focused her thoughts. She looked up at him, meeting his gaze without faltering. 'I'm going to hire another locum,' she said with determination.

He nodded. 'Sounds logical.'

The moment had passed and Kirsten relaxed a little. 'I've

been thinking about it for a while now. Melissa needs me and I want to spend time with her—especially during the next few months.'

'Naturally.' He paused for a moment before asking, 'Did you know you were her guardian?'

'Yes. Jacqui asked me not long after Melissa was born. She's a gorgeous child and looks just like her mother. I really feel for her and it's not surprising she's withdrawn completely from everyone and everything. Her little world has been turned upside down.'

'Is there any other family?'

'Jacqui's brother was killed along with her parents in a light plane crash. Apart from that, I think her husband had a brother but they hadn't spoken in years. In fact, I don't think Jacqui had ever met him.'

'Well, at least Melissa has you, your brothers and your parents.'

'Mmm.' Kirsten looked down at her hands, which she was clenching, before returning to meet his gaze. 'But is it going to be enough?'

Their gazes held and Joel reached out to take her hand in his. He squeezed it gently. 'Time is a great healer, Kirsten. Time and love. With that type of prescription, you can't go wrong.'

Kirsten smiled at him, her gaze blurring with fresh tears. 'Thank you.'

He let go of her hand and signalled for the waiter. 'Now, how about some chocolate fondue? Guaranteed to brush away melancholy and bring an air of happiness.'

'Sounds great.'

Joel ordered for them in French again and when the waiter had gone, Kirsten asked, 'How many languages do you speak?'

'Three, excluding English. It's no big deal. When you travel as much as I do, you pick up the basics. Besides, I was based in Switzerland for almost two years and they speak a variety of German, French and Italian.'

'What was your favourite place in Switzerland?'

His smile was reminiscent. 'Definitely Davos.'

'Lots of good memories?'

He laughed. 'You could say that.'

'Really? What was her name?'

He laughed again and waggled his index finger at her. 'I'm not one to kiss and tell,' he said. The smile slowly faded and Kirsten watched as Joel looked down at the white linen tablecloth. 'Sylvia,' he said, the word barely audible.

The waiter chose that moment to bring their fondue. Kirsten was surprised at the brief surge of jealousy she experienced at the thought of anyone but her kissing Joel McElroy. She fought it immediately, determined to enjoy being with him.

He continued to entertain her with more of his skiing anecdotes, which kept them both laughing until it was time to leave. Kirsten paid the bill before they started the walk back to her car. The weather outside had turned cool and Kirsten pulled her thin jacket around her.

'Would you like my jacket?' Joel asked, and started taking it off.

'No, it's fine.' Her words stopped him. 'Thanks for offering, though.' When they reached her car, Kirsten unlocked the driver's door, realising she was very tired. The last thing she felt like doing was driving. Joel must have seen her fatigue.

'Would you like me to drive?'

'No, I'll be fine. My dear old car is quite temperamental. I'm sure it should require a special licence.'

He chuckled and waited for her to unlock the passenger door.

'Is your knee sore?' Kirsten asked as she started the drive home.

'A bit. It generally aches at the end of the day.'

She nodded. 'I noticed you were limping slightly on the walk to the car.' When he didn't venture anything further, she asked, 'How did you hurt it? I know it was in a skiing accident but would you mind telling me?'

'No. I don't mind.'

Kirsten waited.

'It happened on a Saturday night, well, early evening. It was almost dark and I was heading back to the chalet. I heard a high-pitched scream and saw a flash of hot pink out of the corner of my eye. Just as well her ski-suit was bright and colourful or I might not have seen her so clearly. It had started to snow quite heavily and the poor girl was out of control. She was going much too fast and I knew I needed to slow her down or she'd end up in a mess. I took off after her and managed to get alongside her. I was going to slow her down easily, but when she saw me she lunged at me, taking us both down together.'

He stopped and breathed in deeply. Kirsten looked across at him. His head was back against the seat and his eyes were closed.

'I could see we were heading for a chairlift pylon, but the way we were facing her head would have hit first and at that speed…' He trailed off. He opened his eyes and looked out at the artificially illuminated road ahead. 'Somehow, I have no idea how, I managed to swivel us around just before we hit. My right leg and the left side of her body took the brunt of the collision.'

'And you smashed your knee.'

'My knee, my tibia, my fibula and broke three of my toes. But, as Jed pointed out, it could have been a lot worse. He told me afterwards that when he first heard the list of my injuries, he was very concerned about my knee. If I had required total knee reconstruction, there was no way I would even have stood a chance of trying out for the team.

It'll be twelve weeks tomorrow since the accident, and although it hasn't been an easy three months I have the determination—'

'And stubbornness,' Kirsten couldn't resist interjecting.

Joel smiled. '*And* stubbornness, definitely, to see it through. The knee is slowly getting better. When you offered me the job so close to the Institute of Australasian Sport, where I could continue training, it was impossible to refuse. Having the equipment and physios there, working with me, it will hopefully improve at a more steady pace. That's the main reason I was looking around for part-time work. I need to concentrate on getting my knee better in time for selection for the next Olympic team.'

Kirsten ignored the lump of lead that settled over her heart at his words. She'd always known he'd be leaving. When she'd offered him the job, he'd stated that the recovery of his knee would be his first priority. 'When's that?'

'Next weekend.'

'Will your knee be ready in time?' Kirsten asked with concern.

'I hope so. I spoke to the coach a few weeks ago and he said I need the physio's evaluation to say I'll be ready in time for the Olympics. So keep your fingers crossed.'

Kirsten nodded. 'I'll do that.' Even though she would love to see him stay in Canberra, she'd known for years that Joel's heart was on those slopes. His whole family knew it and accepted it. She'd once listened to Sally talk about winning her Olympic gold, and Kirsten had realised the level of commitment athletes had to have. Drive, commitment and stamina, as well as being a good sports person. That was what Sally had said was needed for a career as a professional athlete and, from what she could see, Joel had all of that—in abundance.

As Kirsten pulled into her driveway, she pressed the re-

mote control for her garage door. After she'd parked the
car inside and switched off the engine, she undid her seat
belt and turned to face him. 'I hope I didn't...' She stopped
and tried again. 'When I asked about the accident, I didn't
mean to cause you any additional pain by reflecting on what
had happened.'

'You didn't,' he replied.

'Good.' Their eyes met and Kirsten swallowed over the
sudden dryness in her throat before saying, 'Thank you for
such a lovely evening. It was fun.'

'It was.' Joel undid his seat belt and leaned towards her,
his hand coming up to cup her cheek. 'You're a very beautiful woman, Kirsten.'

The look in his eyes sent a ripple of delight throughout
her body and Kirsten realised that Joel was about to kiss
her. Her breathing became shallow as her gaze flicked from
his eyes to his mouth, watching in anticipation as his own
lips parted, his face drawing closer and closer. Finally, she
could feel his breath fan lightly across her neck and she
shifted slightly to allow him easier access to her mouth.

When their lips were only millimetres apart, Kirsten
reached out her hand to touch his face, to hurry the agon-
ising slowness of the motion. Her elbow pressed against
the horn, startling both of them. Joel hit his head on the
rear-view mirror and Kirsten hit hers on the back of the
seat.

'Ouch.' He chuckled as he rubbed his head.

'Sorry.'

'You all right?' When she nodded, he continued, 'I think
there may be a more comfortable way to kiss you goodnight.' With that, he opened his door, collecting his briefcase as he went.

Kirsten sat there for a second, just watching him, his
words registering. Joel wanted to kiss her goodnight. Joel
wanted to *kiss* her. Her body zinged to life at the thought.

When her sluggish brain caught up with the situation, she realised that the sooner she hurried up and went inside, the sooner he would be kissing her.

After collecting her handbag and medical bag, Kirsten locked the car and headed for the door that led through to her laundry. Thankfully, she'd remembered to set the timer for her heating to come on so the house was nice and warm. She continued on into the kitchen where Joel had put his briefcase down and shed his jacket.

She looked at him, uncertain what to do next. After putting her bags down, she nervously turned to fill the kettle. 'Tea?' she asked, and her voice cracked on the word. Joel waited until she was finished before he held out a hand to her.

'Come here,' he said softly as he leaned back against the bench. Kirsten took the few steps that separated them and gently placed her hand into his outstretched one. Joel gathered her close and held her firmly to his chest, her body fitting his with perfection.

Kirsten listened to the beating of his heart, the steady rhythm calming her own down to a normal pace. They must have stood there for at least five full minutes, just relaxing within each other's arms.

Joel leaned back a little and Kirsten did the same, gazing up into the blue eyes that had frequented her dreams during the past week. 'What's the name of your perfume?' he asked, his voice husky. 'It's been driving me insane all week long.'

Kirsten smiled up at him. 'Insayne,' she told him, and he shook his head slightly in disbelief.

'I should have guessed.'

With that, Joel leaned down to claim her mouth with his own. Kirsten closed her eyes and held her breath, waiting with desperate anticipation for that first moment when his lips would brush against hers.

When it finally happened, she breathed out on a sigh of contentment. If Joel had needed any further encouragement, that was it. Her mouth tasted sweet and glorious, just as he'd known it would. He'd fantasised all week about how it would feel to hold her in his arms once more, to kiss her as he was doing now, and his fantasies had been no match for the reality of Kirsten.

The kisses started off soft and slow, the desire deep within her slowly mounting. When his tongue brushed lightly against her lower lip, Kirsten shuddered and groaned, opening her mouth to him.

As though flicking a switch, the passion which had been carefully controlled simultaneously burst forth from both of them. Kirsten plunged her fingers into his hair, something she'd been desperate to do since his first night there. Joel's arms tightened around her, their bodies now pressed firmly against each other.

His hands touched her long braid impatiently and Kirsten's senses realised what he wanted. Without breaking lip contact, she eased back, her hands quickly finding the end of her braid and roughly pulling the band out.

Within seconds, her hair was free as Joel ran his fingers through the long auburn tresses. Kirsten placed her hands on his cheeks and pulled back momentarily. She gazed up at him, his eyes glazed with desire. They were both gasping but the instant their breathing started to slow, Joel plundered her mouth once more.

The feelings of passion spiralled higher and higher until at last Joel broke off, only to trail hot kisses along Kirsten's neck. She tipped her head to the side, allowing him access, goose-bumps spreading like wildfire over her body.

'Mmm,' she groaned, and closed her eyes, savouring the sensation. 'Joel,' she whispered.

'Hmm?' he said as his lips met hers again, once, twice,

three times, before he pulled back and looked down into her upturned face.

'That's the most...*incredible*...goodnight kiss I've ever had.'

A slow and sexy smile spread across his mouth. 'Me, too.'

CHAPTER FOUR

WHEN Kirsten woke the next morning, it was with the memory of Joel's passionate kisses uppermost in her mind. She sighed and snuggled into the pillow beside her. He had kissed her a few more times before setting her from him and heading for the door.

There, he'd kissed her once more and said goodnight. He was a gentleman and he was utterly charming. Kirsten kept telling herself to watch out or she'd be falling in love with him, but when he was around it was easier to throw caution to the wind and just enjoy being with him. He made her feel alive, vibrant and very feminine. He'd helped her through the depression she'd been experiencing at the loss of her cousin and now, thanks to him, she felt better equipped to cope with the grieving four-year-old due to arrive in two weeks' time.

There was a knock at the side door and Kirsten quickly jumped out of bed and pulled on her robe and slippers before padding out to the kitchen. Opening the curtain, she looked directly into Dr Joel McElroy's blue eyes.

'Good morning,' she said after opening the door, a wide smile on her face. She moved aside and urged him in out of the wet and cold Canberra morning into the warmth of her home before closing the door behind him. Kirsten looked at him again and realised that he wasn't smiling. 'Something wrong?' she asked, a strange, heavy feeling settling over her.

'No. Ready to go?' He forced a smile and his tone was polite—*too* polite.

Where was the man from last night? she wondered as

the heavy feeling turned to dread as she read Joel's body language. He was rigid and controlled. Any thoughts she might have had of a good morning hug and kiss were blown away with the breeze outside.

He was dressed in a suit with his coat draped over his arm and his briefcase in hand. Everything about him said business and business only!

'Um…' Kirsten swallowed and turned away. 'What time is it?'

'Time we were heading for the hospital,' he replied. 'You have…' he consulted his watch '…exactly ten minutes to shower, dress and be in the car before we're officially late for our first day on the emergency roster.' Again his tone was polite.

She frowned. 'I didn't think we started until ten o'clock.' As she said the words, she glanced at the kitchen clock, her eyes widening as she realised the time. 'Oh, my goodness. It's twenty minutes to ten!'

'I know.' He watched as she frantically looked around for something to tie her hair back with. He spied a hairband on the floor, and as he bent to pick it up he realised it was the same one she'd ripped out of her hair the previous night.

'Will this do?' The memory of running his fingers through her hair caused a tightening in his gut.

'Yes, thank you.' Her tone was a little stiff as she took the band from him, and he knew his aloofness was responsible for her change in mood.

'You're not going to wash it?' he asked as she hurried out of the room. Moments later she walked passed him, her arms full of clothes.

'Do you have any idea how long it takes to wash and dry my hair? A *long* time,' she continued, not giving him time to respond. 'Today is one of those days when I desperately want to cut it,' she mumbled as she headed towards the bathroom.

'Don't!' The vehemence of the word surprised him more than it did her. She stopped and looked at him for a moment, a puzzled frown creasing her forehead, before she continued on her way.

Joel closed his eyes and rubbed his fingers across his forehead. He *had* to keep his distance from her. He heard the shower start and forced himself not to think about her standing naked beneath the warm spray, only a short distance away.

Last night, he'd let things go too far and now he was regretting it—regretting the way Kirsten made him feel, as well as the way he'd just squashed her happiness like a bug. The least he could do was make amends by fixing her some tea and toast.

'But that's all,' he said quietly to himself as he switched the kettle on and put the bread into the toaster.

Last night... Joel groaned and raked his hand through his hair as the memories returned. Last night he'd been unable to control the need to kiss her. By taking her in his arms and pressing his lips against hers, Joel had discovered one important fact—that Kirsten Doyle kissed like a dream. He could quite easily become addicted to her...and he really didn't have the time for it. Not with Olympic selection just around the corner. Besides, if he *did* do something about the attraction between them, he'd be prising open all the old wounds that had taken the last three years to heal. Three long and lonely years since Sylvia's death.

Five minutes later, Kirsten emerged, dressed in khaki trousers and a white knit top with matching cardigan. She carried her handbag which she was frantically checking. 'Lipstick. I can't find my lipstick.' Without another word, she dumped her bag on the bench and rushed back to her room, her loose hair flying out behind her.

When she returned, she grabbed for the toast. 'Thanks for breakfast.'

She was gorgeous, he thought as he watched her, and in more ways than one. Joel couldn't resist smiling. 'I'm guessing you've slept in before.'

Kirsten nodded and sipped at her tea. 'Yup.' She took another bite. He realised this was a rare privilege and insight, seeing Kirsten not only in a fluster but frantically getting ready. Generally, when people were in a hurry, they didn't worry too much about pomp and ceremony.

She flicked her hair back, slung her handbag on her shoulder, drained her cup, picked up the last piece of toast and started locking up the house.

'Let's go,' she mumbled with her mouth half-full. As she walked around, her gaze was searching the bench, the floor and the table. When she finally looked at Joel, he read panic in her eyes.

He held up his hand, the car keys dangling from his fingers. 'Looking for these?'

She swallowed her mouthful. 'Yes.' She held out her hand for them.

'I'll drive today,' he announced as he headed towards the laundry. 'That way, you can do your hair and put your make-up on calmly, instead of doing it at the red lights.'

Kirsten was a bit irritated at his high-handedness but knew that this morning he was probably right. 'You can always tell a man who has sisters,' she mumbled.

Joel laughed and went out the door into the garage. Soon he was heading towards Canberra General Hospital, after Kirsten had given him several instructions on how to handle her temperamental clutch and gear lever.

'Here,' she grumbled as she flicked the windscreen wiper lever to a higher speed. 'You can hardly see the road with that much rain on the window,' she rationalised when he glared at her.

'I think I should have made you an extra piece of toast,' he said as Kirsten started putting her make-up on.

'There are other ways of keeping me quiet than just stuffing food into my mouth.' The instant the words were said, she realised the *double entendre*. All she'd meant was that he should just ask her to keep quiet, but she knew from the slight rise of his eyebrows that he thought she was referring to the kisses they'd shared.

'I know.' His tone was matter-of-fact but his knuckles were almost white as his hands tightened on the wheel.

Something is definitely wrong, she thought, before concentrating on the task at hand. One minute he was happy and the next he was frowning with such intensity he'd permanently crease his brow if the wind suddenly changed. Once her make-up was on, she set about doing her hair, which wasn't easy in the car. She flicked Joel once and mumbled an apology before swivelling slightly to allow better access for braiding her hair.

'I guess you always have it that way because it's quick and easy,' he suggested.

'That and the fact that it stays and looks neater,' she answered crisply and Joel knew he'd squashed that spark again. He shook his head.

'Do you always wear trousers?'

'What's with the criticisms?' she asked a little hotly.

'I wasn't criticising,' he replied quickly. 'Just asking a question.'

Kirsten sighed. 'Fine. I like trousers better than skirts. That's it. In summer, I wear shorts. I've never been a dress or skirt type of person, although I have nothing against the garments.'

'I've never been a dress or skirt type person either,' he told her, his teasing gaze encompassing her.

'Glad to hear it,' she teased back, and he was glad he'd

made her smile again. 'Ooh, go left here,' she said, pointing. 'It's easier to get into the doctors' car park this way.'

Joel followed the directions she gave him, and when they arrived at the boom gate she gave him the code to allow them access. They walked into Accident and Emergency with one whole minute to spare.

'Well done, Dr Doyle,' he whispered in her ear, and Kirsten not only felt pride at his comment but quickly had to control the increase in her pulse rate at his close proximity. They were greeted by Renee, the triage sister, who showed them where to put their bags and coats.

'Still raining?' she asked.

'Yes,' they answered in unison.

'That means a busy day for us all,' Renee surmised. She was just about to show Kirsten and Joel around when Alex walked into A and E.

'Hi, there, brother-in-law-to-be,' he said, shaking Joel's hand warmly. 'How's the knee?'

'Progressing,' Joel answered with a smile. 'Slowly but surely.'

'Tib and fib?'

'All healed. You should have received a report from the orthopaedic surgeon you referred me to in Sydney, as well as a report from not only my sister but probably my mother as well,' Joel replied.

'I have but it's also good to hear it from the patient's perspective.' Alex turned to Kirsten and kissed her cheek. 'You're looking as lovely as ever,' he told her. 'Jordanne and I are on call today for orthopaedics. She's in the ward at the moment but should be here—'

'Right now,' Jordanne said from behind him. She gave her fiancé a quick hug before turning to her brother. 'Obviously Kirsten's been working you hard this week. This is the first time I've seen you since you arrived.' She wrapped her arms around her brother and kissed his cheek. 'I'm glad you're here,' she said.

Kirsten felt a little uncomfortable being around Jordanne. Was it obvious to her friend that she and Joel had been kissing? Not that she thought Jordanne would be upset—probably quite the contrary—but Kirsten had never told her about the infatuation she'd had with Joel.

'Have we finished with the family reunion?' Renee asked with a laugh. 'Just as well Jed and Sally are in Sydney this weekend.'

Jordanne simply smiled before turning to Alex. 'As Jed is away this weekend and you're responsible for his patients, a message was sent down from the burns unit to the orthopaedic ward that Ian Behr would like a word with you,' she told him.

'How is he this morning?' Kirsten asked.

'He's getting there,' Jordanne responded.

'Good. I spoke to Stephanie, his mother, every day last week and she seems to be coping better now that he's off the critical list.'

'The whole situation would have been a lot worse had you two not been there to help.'

'I think we're all grateful that Stephanie decided to come to my house before doing anything else,' Kirsten replied.

'Anyway,' Alex said, 'we'd better go and see if anything's troubling him.'

When they'd gone, Renee started the ball rolling. 'I know you were both in for orientation earlier on in the week but let me take you quickly through it again while everything is quiet. Over here,' she pointed to a big whiteboard, 'is the daily roster. This tells you which consultant is on call for the different departments. Trauma rooms one and two...' Renee indicated the rooms that were set up for emergencies '...and over here are the treatment rooms. Basically, you'll be seeing people who present at A and E with a variety of ailments. If you have problems finding things, just ask one of the nurses.' Renee headed back to her desk and pulled out two identification badges. 'Here are the results of the lovely photographs you had taken the other day.'

'Nice one,' Joel said as he looked at Kirsten's photo.

'Yours isn't so bad either,' she told him, and wished she could somehow get her hands on a copy of it. He was very photogenic, she realised as she watched him clip the badge on.

'When an emergency comes in, you'll only be required to help out if we're short-staffed. Your main focus is to clear the waiting-room of patients,' she finished. 'Questions?'

'Not a single one,' Joel said and Kirsten shook her head.

'Right, then. Let's get started.' Renee introduced them to the other doctors who were currently seeing patients before handing them each a patient file.

Kirsten was surprised at how quickly the time flew. She only ran into a few obstacles, mainly not being able to find some of the equipment she needed. That was soon rectified with help from one of the nurses, and two hours later Kirsten went out into the A and E waiting-room to find it empty.

'How did it go?' Joel's deep voice asked from behind her, and Kirsten swung around, looking immediately up into his smiling eyes.

'Great. You?'

'Good.' He took a deep breath. 'As much as I love to ski, I also love helping people out.'

'I know what you mean, even though I generally had hay-fever problems that were slightly exacerbated because people had waited too long before seeing a doctor.'

'It's always the way, though. As soon as the weekend

comes and the general doctors' surgeries aren't open, then up to the hospital they come.'

'Kids getting things stuck in their ears and minor burns from an overturned coffee-cup *always* happens at the most inappropriate hour,' she agreed.

'Speaking of coffee, do you think we have time for a quick cup now?'

'I don't see why not but let's just double check with Renee first,' Kirsten suggested, and they went in search of the triage sister.

'By all means, have a break while you can,' Renee told them as she put the phone down. 'We've just had a call from the police to say there's been a three-car pile-up on the Parkway. I hate rainy days,' she grumbled, but continued, 'Ambulances are on their way and should be here within the hour so it may be a good time to have lunch as well because you can bet that the instant those emergencies arrive a flood of minor ailments are going to come through the door.'

Joel and Kirsten decided to take Renee at her word and headed for the cafeteria where they also found Alex and Jordanne.

'Eat up,' Alex told them when they had sat down with their food. 'The rest of the afternoon looks to be pretty hectic.' They talked about a multitude of topics while they ate.

'I guess you don't have any details yet of the pile-up,' Kirsten said as she glanced at the clock on the wall. It had been almost half an hour since Renee had received that phone call.

'No, but we should be getting a report through soon,' Alex said, before turning to Joel. 'By the way, Joel, Jordanne said you hold a diploma in general surgery. Is that correct?'

Kirsten had often toyed with the idea of taking a diploma

but, with building up her practice and now Melissa coming, she didn't really have the time. And to be honest, she'd never really been in a position to need the extra skills. If any of her patients required surgical intervention, it was usually on a referral from her to a surgeon or they presented at A and E. She waited for Joel to finish his mouthful so he could answer.

'Yes, but I haven't done any operating for over three years,' he replied, his tone soft.

Kirsten watched as his gaze met Jordanne's—brother and sister shared a knowing look.

'Why do you think I'm here?' he asked, spreading his arms wide. 'To refresh my skills and learn something knew.'

'You're never too old to learn,' Jordanne quoted their mother in a very good imitation of Jane McElroy's voice.

Joel laughed. 'Exactly.'

'It's all right,' Alex said. 'I'm not asking you to operate this afternoon but it's good to know these things in case we need it.' His pager sounded and Jordanne groaned. 'It's A and E.'

'We'd better be going, then,' Jordanne said as she drained her cup. The four of them went back to A and E and reported to Renee.

'News?' Alex asked, and they all listened closely while Renee read the report just in from the paramedics.

'Sounds as though we're going to be in Theatre for a while,' Jordanne said. 'I'll head off to Theatres and start getting the equipment organised.'

'Trust Jed and Sally to pick this weekend to go to Sydney,' Alex grumbled, before following his fiancée.

'I guess we'll get back to the waiting-room, unless you need us elsewhere,' Joel said as he and Kirsten left Renee to do her job in peace. As Renee had predicted, they had a flood of patients arrive, some connected with the car accident and others just in for some advice or help.

Kirsten had one twenty-year-old man who complained of extreme pain on the lower right hand side of his abdomen. She immediately thought it was appendicitis—indeed, he exhibited all the symptoms—but when she quizzed him on his past medical history, he told her that his appendix had been removed when he was eight. She gave him some pain relief and ordered a blood test. Knowing the general surgical registrar would be busy with the motor-vehicle accident, she decided to ask Joel for a second opinion.

'You think it's appendicitis?'

'All of the symptoms are classic but he's sure he had it out when he was eight years old.'

'It may be gastroenteritis or a bowel obstruction, but the blood test will reveal more.' After Joel had finished examining the patient, they both agreed to send the young man for an ultrasound, which would hopefully show up any abnormalities in the area.

They were both in treatment room two after the orderly had taken their patient to Radiology. 'Well, while we're waiting on the results of that,' Kirsten said, 'and things are quiet for the moment, I might just go to the burns unit and see how Ian's doing for myself. Is that all right with you?'

'Sure. I'll ring through there if you're needed,' Joel told her.

Kirsten left A and E and walked to the burns unit. She introduced herself to the ward sister then crossed to Ian's bedside where Stephanie was sitting.

'Hello, neighbours. You're looking better, Ian,' she told him as she had a quick look at his chart.

'Feeling better.' He smiled gratefully at her. 'Thanks, Kirsten. Mum says I might have...' He choked up and tears welled in his eyes. Stephanie shushed him but he continued,

'I just wanted to say thanks and tell that to the other doctor who was helping you.'

'I'll pass the message on,' she told him. She stayed and chatted for another five minutes before the ward sister came across to let her know that A and E had called for her to return. 'Sorry,' she told them. 'Duty calls. I'll try and get in to see you some time next week but, I confess, I'm looking forward to seeing you at home instead of in hospital.' She smiled at him.

'Me, too,' Ian replied.

When Kirsten arrived back in A and E, Joel had a look of disbelief on his face. 'What's wrong?' she asked.

'There's been another accident.'

'Another car crash?'

'No.' His face was solemn. 'There's been a mud slide at one of the alpine villages. Cabins and trees have been flattened.'

'What!' Kirsten couldn't believe it. She shook her head. 'So much for a relaxing first day on the job!'

'Renee has just paged the news through to Alex who's in Theatre. He's head of the hospital's retrieval team,' Joel told her. 'They are so short-staffed around here that I'm not sure who Alex is going to send.'

'How's the ailment status?' she asked, gesturing to the empty waiting-room.

'Exactly as it looks. I sincerely hope it's not the calm before the storm, if you'll pardon the pun.'

'So that means we can help out somewhere else.' Just as Kirsten had finished talking, Renee came up. 'What's happening, Renee?'

'Alex is going to hand over to Jordanne who has, incidentally, just walked into Theatre two from Theatre one. He'll be out in a minute to put his retrieval team together.' She looked at Joel. 'He said he wants you on it as you know the area quite well. Don't you?' Renee asked, not too sure.

'It's the same area he pulled me from three months ago,' Joel agreed with a nod.

'Good. Kirsten, would you mind keeping things in the waiting-room under control? That may mean taking down patient details and getting them to fill in forms because we're short-staffed. I've called a few of my nurses in but it will take them a while to get here. Alex will be holding a briefing in the doctors' tea-room in ten minutes. Joel, can you make sure you're there, please.'

'Certainly.'

'Right. That's you two organised.' With that, Renee took off in the direction she had come from.

Kirsten turned to look at Joel. 'It makes sense, Alex wanting to take you along. Are you nervous?'

'Why would I be?' he asked. 'I've been involved with rescue parties in avalanches, mud slides and all sorts of skiing mishaps for years, Kirsten. Alex is right. I do know the terrain and the regular people who work there.'

Even though they were standing out near the waiting-room reception desk, Kirsten put her hand on his arm and squeezed gently. She didn't care who, if anyone, saw. 'Please, be careful,' she said to him, worry in her gaze.

'I will,' he assured her. 'After all the scrapes and trouble I've been in over the years, this should be a cinch.' Joel smiled down at her and Kirsten's insides turned to mush. 'Everything will be fine,' he said softly.

'Excuse me, miss,' an elderly lady was saying from the other side of the desk. Kirsten turned and looked at her before glancing back at Joel.

'I'll come and say goodbye before we go,' Joel promised, and walked away. Kirsten took a deep breath and returned her attention to the patient, a smile plastered firmly in place.

'What can I do for you?'

'It's my husband,' the lady said. 'He's out in our car and he can't get out. I think he's done his back in.'

'OK.' Kirsten looked around for an orderly but found the area completely empty except for herself and the patient. 'Right, then, let's get a wheelchair and go and take a look at your husband.' She went around to where the woman was standing. 'I'm Dr Doyle,' she said, and the worried look on the woman's face disappeared.

'It seems very quiet here,' the woman said as she followed Kirsten over to where the orderlies kept the wheelchairs. Kirsten looked around for the register and signed the chair out. She also grabbed one of the large hospital umbrellas that were standing in a bucket in the corner.

'There are a few emergencies,' Kirsten explained.

'I didn't know you were a doctor. You're not wearing a white coat.'

Kirsten smiled as she headed for the outside doors. 'We don't wear white coats all the time,' she replied. The sudden blast of cold air hit Kirsten with force, the old lady was bundled up in her thick coat.

'Where did you park your car?' Kirsten asked.

'It's over there, in the disabled parking spot. I know I probably shouldn't have parked there but I didn't want to be too far away from the entrance, especially in this rain.'

'Good thinking,' Kirsten said, and wheeled the chair under shelter for as long as she could. When she was parallel with the car, she turned to the woman. 'Stay here with the chair while I take a look at your husband.'

The elderly woman nodded. Kirsten put the umbrella up and walked across, knocking briefly on the door, not wanting to startle the man too much, and gently opened the door.

'Hello. I'm Dr Doyle. I understand you're in a bit of pain?'

'Yes. I've done my back in,' he groaned.

'Is this a recurring injury?'

'Yes. The last time I did it, I was bedridden for weeks, you know.'

'I see,' Kirsten replied with a smile. 'Well Mr…'

'Muller,' he supplied.

'Mr Muller, I'll help you out of the car and into the wheelchair before we whisk you inside where it's nice and warm. How does that sound?'

'An improvement on my present predicament,' Mr Muller replied.

Kirsten told him how she would move him before getting the chair into position. She asked Mrs Muller to come and hold the umbrella for them so they didn't all get drenched. No wonder there had been a mud slide, she mused as she assisted Mr Muller into the chair. With all this rain they'd been having and the thawing of a large amount of snow that had lasted well into October, a mud slide was probably just sitting around *waiting* to happen.

Kirsten took the Mullers inside and wheeled Mr Muller into treatment room one, noticing that there still weren't any other patients waiting to be seen—thank goodness.

After she'd examined Mr Muller's back, she organised for an X-ray and took him and his wife down to Radiology. When she returned, it was to find Joel looking for her.

'I'm here,' she said, a smile instantly appearing on her face. 'I was worried that I might have missed you.' She urged him to follow her into one of the treatment rooms. If he was going to kiss her goodbye, which she sincerely hoped he was, she wanted it to be in private. 'How did the briefing go?'

'OK. There are twenty-five people still trapped and emergencies crews from Cooma are attending the scene, but there's one woman—Frances Althorpe is her name—who is badly injured. The paramedics at the site haven't been able to give a clear estimate of her wounds as she's still half-trapped by very unstable rubble.'

'Joel, that's terrible. When do you leave?'

'*We*,' he said, pointing from her to him and back again.

'Pardon?'

'Alex is one pair of hands short on his retrieval team and sent me to tell you that you've just been drafted.'

'But...' Kirsten spluttered. 'But I don't know the first thing about retrieval procedures.'

'Then I guess you're going to learn fast because there isn't anyone else,' he said as he reached for her hand. But she stepped back.

'Hasn't Renee called in extra staff? What about the waiting area here? It's Saturday afternoon and it's raining. Don't a lot of kids play sport on Saturdays? And what if they all get hurt? There will be no one in A and E to fix them,' she protested, her mind reeling with apprehension about going on a retrieval.

'Come with me. We can talk as we go.' Joel took her hand in his and walked her out of the treatment room. 'You were brilliant the other night when we had Ian's emergency.'

'Yes, but it's not something I'm used to doing on a grand scale such as this,' she pointed out.

'With regard to A and E, Renee has everything under control. Give her a brief report on the patients you've already seen and their whereabouts. They're getting the helicopter ready to fly us to Jindabine and then we go by car up to the accident site. That way it should only take us about an hour to get there, instead of the three-and-a-bit-hour drive—even more with the conditions being so bad.'

'But—'

'There's no time for buts, Kirsten.' Joel squeezed her hand encouragingly. She could tell he was pumped up with adrenalin at the thought of helping to rescue people and now it was spilling over onto her. 'You can do it. I'll help you.'

She drew in a deep breath and pushed away the doubts. Alex and Joel would be there with her and it wasn't as though she were being asked to perform lifesaving surgery on someone. She was just an extra pair of hands, to carry the equipment or do whatever it was that was needed. Right?

CHAPTER FIVE

WRONG! Kirsten watched the ground beneath her loom closer as she was winched down through the large cavern of rubble. The emergency services had been working hard for the past four hours and now that daylight was beginning to slip away, the urgency of the situation had increased.

'You're almost there, Kirsten,' Alex's voice said in her headset.

During the trip to the accident site, she had listened intently to what Alex had said regarding the situation. When they'd arrived, she'd done whatever they'd asked until Joel and Alex had stood together, talking quietly, before crossing to her side. She relived the moment that had brought her to this place in time.

'How much do you weigh?' Joel had asked, and Kirsten had known this was no time to tease him about asking rude questions.

'Sixty-four kilograms,' she'd answered hesitantly. 'Why?' As soon as she'd asked the question, she hadn't been at all sure she'd wanted to know the answer.

'The volunteer fire brigade unit who initially found Frances had difficulty staying with her as the rubble beside her was unstable. It was still sleeting then but now that the rain has thankfully stopped for a while, we want to try to get down to her again. She previously regained consciousness, which is how we know her name, and one of the volunteers was a trained paramedic. He set up an IV line and administered morphine. Right now, though, we need a medically trained person to go down who is light enough not to disturb the area too much,' Joel had explained.

Kirsten must have had a look of sheer terror on her face because Joel had quickly placed his arm about her shoulders and given them a little squeeze. 'You'll be fine. You'll be in a safety harness, attached to a winch, and we can get you out of there at any time.'

'You'll also be in constant radio contact with me,' Alex added. 'You can do it, Kirsten.'

'All right,' she said, drawing confidence from both of them, feeling as though there was no other option. After all, a woman's life was at stake.

'Excellent.' Alex went to make the arrangements.

'Close your eyes,' Joel commanded softly when they were alone. Kirsten just looked at him before realising he was serious. Surely he wasn't going to kiss her in front of all of these people? Slowly she closed her eyes. 'Now, take a deep breath,' he continued. Kirsten complied. 'Right, let it out slowly and give your arms a little shake. Open your eyes.'

When she did so he looked down into her upturned face. 'Feel any better?'

'Not really.' Her insides were still churning over at the thought of being winched down to the patient below. She felt sick and wasn't sure whether she could go through with it.

Joel turned her to him and pressed his lips firmly to her own. Kirsten closed her eyes, blocking out everything around her except Joel and the feel of his lips against hers. Her head started to spin as his lips moved over hers. She sighed into the kiss and wrapped her arms around his back, drawing strength from the embrace.

He gently eased away. 'How about now?' he asked, his breathing as uneven as hers.

Kirsten recalled looking up into the amazing depths of his beautiful blue eyes and relaxing for the first time since she'd arrived on the scene. 'Definitely,' she'd whispered.

Before she'd known what was happening, she was being winched down towards Frances Althorpe, the emergency medical kit strapped to her front, ready and waiting to be used. Finally, Kirsten touched the broken slabs of concrete and debris with her foot.

'I'm down,' she said into her headset. They'd put her a few metres from Frances and, still attached, Kirsten carefully picked her way over. 'Frances?' she said firmly, as she knelt beside the patient's head and upper arm, which were exposed. 'Frances? I'm Dr Doyle. I'm here to help you.'

Kirsten received no reply from the patient and quickly took out her medical torch to check the pupils. 'Pupils still reacting to light,' she said into her headset as she continued with her other observations.

'Has the rubble you're standing on moved?' Alex asked.

'No. It's stable. Pulse is weak.'

'Internal bleeding!' Alex mumbled.

'Yes,' Kirsten agreed.

'How's the IV line going?'

'Almost finished. I'll swap the bag over.' Once Kirsten had done that and her patient's obs had all been recorded by Alex, she said, 'I'm going to try and move some of these smaller pieces away.'

'Be careful,' he warned.

Heeding Alex's advice, she picked up a few pieces and carefully put them down away from Frances. The wind was cold but at least the rain had stopped—for now. 'Frances?' Kirsten called again and still received no reply. 'I'm just trying to…' Kirsten lifted a heavy piece of brick and carefully placed it on the ground '…move some of this debris away,' she continued, trying hard not to shift her weight around too much.

'Kirsten?'

'Yes, Alex?'

'I'm going to send Joel down. From what we can see and from what you're doing, the debris seems to have settled a bit more.'

'OK. It's quite dry now,' she said, but kept on with her task. Soon Joel was carefully winched down. 'Long time, no see,' she said.

'Having fun?' he asked ironically.

'Actually, Joel, I can't say that I am but it's not as bad as I'd thought it would be.' Kirsten stopped moving the debris and checked Frances's vital signs again. 'Same,' she reported.

Slowly, they managed to move most of the debris from around Frances's torso but her lower half was still buried. As Joel was definitely more experienced in retrieval procedures, Kirsten deferred to his judgement.

'You just like bossing me around,' she quipped as they continued the painstakingly slow job of removing the debris. Piece by piece and bit by bit was the only way they were going to get Frances out of there.

'Yes, I confess I do,' he said with a smile. 'Why don't you do her obs again, Dr Doyle?'

'Is that a request or an order, Dr McElroy?' she replied sweetly.

'Please,' Joel said, their gazes holding for a brief second, each careful not to blind the other with the lamps attached to their helmets. Kirsten grinned at him.

'That's better.' She nodded before starting on the obs. 'Frances?' she called, and for the first time since they'd been down there Frances actually stirred. Kirsten glanced briefly at Joel.

'Did you hear that or was it my imagination?'

Joel shook his head, stopped what he was doing and listened. 'Frances?' he called. 'Can you hear me?'

Frances muttered incoherently. Her eyes were still closed

but this time they were clenched tight, showing that she'd regained consciousness.

'Draw up some more morphine. The last she had was well over five hours ago,' Joel instructed as he pulled off his digging gloves, swapping them for a pair of medical gloves. 'Frances, I'm Dr McElroy and this is Dr Doyle. You're trapped beneath some debris, but try not to worry because we're here to help you.' He turned to Kirsten. 'Ready?' he asked.

She nodded and carefully administered the morphine. Within another two minutes Frances had slipped back into unconsciousness and Joel and Kirsten resumed their work.

As more of Frances's body was revealed, they treated her wounds. They splinted her fractured arm and hand, cleaned and bandaged the cuts on her face and were grateful when two more workers were sent down to help with the rubble. The powerful searchlights now shone down on their area as the sun had set.

'Kirsten, Joel.' Alex's voice came through their headsets. 'It's time for you to come back up and rest.'

When they were back on top again, Kirsten felt like collapsing to the ground to rest her weary body. Instead, Joel took her hand in his and led her over to a tent, set up with refreshments for the rescue teams.

They walked into the tent and found it empty. A table of food was set out across the back and some chairs were spaced around the tent. Even though she was wearing a heavy-duty raincoat, Kirsten was glad to be out of the biting wind.

'Exhausting isn't it?' Joel asked rhetorically, before leaning over to squeeze her hand. 'Just wait until we get her out. The elation you'll feel is…incredible.'

'I hope so, Joel, because right now I feel like curling up in a nice warm bed and sleeping for a week.'

He laughed softly. 'I agree.' The smile slid slowly from

his face and Kirsten watched as he stared out into the busy night.

'Have you ever lost a patient out on retrieval?' she asked carefully.

'Yes. In circumstances like that, you need to live with the fact that you did everything—*everything*—possible to help the person.' His words were so vehement that Kirsten wondered if there wasn't more to his words than just helping her through this experience.

'I don't think I want to think about it,' she replied.

'Best not to until you have to,' he said, and took a deep breath. He closed his eyes for a moment, pain and anguish contorting his handsome features.

'Joel?'

He opened his eyes to look into hers. 'Life is far too precious to waste,' he murmured, before reaching forward to kiss her. Her eyelids fluttered closed and she waited with a breathless anticipation for their lips to meet. This kiss wasn't like any other they'd shared. It was soft and pliant as well as being…sad.

As his tongue tenderly caressed her mouth, Kirsten felt a shudder rip through her body which spread goose-bumps over her flesh. She eased closer to him, wrapping her arms about his neck and giving in to the sensations awakening throughout her being.

The leisurely yet masterful strokes of his mouth continued to send her emotions spiralling out of control. His hands were at her waist but even through the raincoat and the overalls she could feel the warmth radiating from his touch.

Kirsten sighed appreciatively and the sound seemed to fuel Joel's fire as the kiss suddenly turned urgent. It was as though he was living out his words—life was far too precious to waste. She matched the intensity of the kiss, urging him on.

With a start he pulled away and looked down at her. She read sorrow in his eyes and instinctively knew this emotion wasn't directed at her. Although he'd been aloof after their first kiss last night, she sensed his present mood had more to do with his past.

Kirsten's breathing was shallow but she returned his gaze. 'What happened?' Her words were soft and for a moment she thought he hadn't heard.

'It was a long time ago,' he whispered, reaching his hand up to caress her cheek, his thumb rubbing gently over her skin. 'You're a very beautiful woman, Kirsten.'

'I'll bet she was beautiful, too,' she stated, without jealousy.

'Yes.' He raked a hand through his hair.

'Want to talk about it?'

'There isn't much to tell.'

'Fair enough,' she replied, and crossed to the table where the sandwiches were. She picked up a packet that contained two sandwiches and cleared her throat. 'Did you want some?'

'Sure.' He came over and looked down at the assortment before choosing. Kirsten helped herself to a cup of coffee and sat down, placing her cup beneath her chair. Joel followed suit. An uncomfortable silence began to stretch between them and Kirsten tried desperately to think of something to say. She hadn't wanted to pressure Joel to talk— far from it. She'd thought he'd *wanted* to talk about Sylvia, who obviously still played a part in his life.

'We were in Switzerland and it was a terrible night.' His quiet words broke the silence.

'Joel,' she interrupted, 'you don't have to tell me if you don't want to. I don't want you to think I'm pressuring you.'

He smiled at her then and the uneasiness she'd previously felt disappeared.

'I want to tell you about Sylvia, Kirsten.' He said this softly and shook his head sadly. 'We'd been out skiing, were late getting back and the blizzard closed in so quickly…' He trailed off. Kirsten held her breath and placed her free hand over his, wanting to be there for him. 'Thankfully, there was an emergency hut nearby. They have them spaced across the snowfields for occasions such as these. They carry basic medical supplies, food, blankets, that type of thing. As we headed in the direction of the hut, Sylvia stumbled and lost her footing. She rolled down a slope, dropped ten metres into a ravine and fell hard against a rock.' Joel's tone was flat. 'I managed to get her to the hut but her internal injuries were extensive. I used what medical supplies I had to try and fix her up but she desperately needed a blood transfusion.' He looked down at their clasped hands then looked up into Kirsten's eyes. 'It was over twenty-four hours later that they found us. Sylvia was buried in Davos three days later. We were due to be married at the end of that month.'

Kirsten sat quietly, absorbing his words. 'It must have been very hard for you.'

'It was, but…' he took a deep breath '…my family have always been there when I needed them and that time was no exception.'

'Families can be good at that—yours especially.' She smiled gently.

Joel squeezed her hand before letting it go. 'It was a long time ago. I'm a different person now from who I was then. Death has a way of changing us.'

She nodded. 'Thank you for sharing this with me.'

He smiled at her. 'Right now, though, I guess we'd better eat up before we're needed again.'

'Good thinking.'

They ate together in a companionable silence, and as

Kirsten was finishing her coffee Alex walked into the tent. 'What's the news?' she asked.

'We're about to move some big slabs of concrete, and from what we can see of the area around Frances's legs she's going to need extensive surgery on them. I'll remain at the top so as soon as she's winched up I can start treating her. I'd like the two of you to go back down and assist with her transfer to the stretcher.'

Kirsten took a deep breath and Alex smiled at her. 'I know this is your first retrieval, Kirsten, and you're doing a great job. The whole team is. The other rescue crews have managed to dig out ten other people—two were dead and the other eight are on their way to Canberra General. Frances is trapped the worst, from what we can tell.'

'Let's get to it, then,' Joel said, and patted Alex's back.

The rain had started again, which slowed everything down, and it was another hour and a half before Joel and Kirsten carefully transferred Frances to the stretcher. She was then carefully winched away from the rubble that had held her captive.

Finally it was over and Kirsten was back on solid ground once more. Alex, his registrar and two nurses were attending to Frances's injuries.

'You head back with Alex,' Joel said to her as he came up behind her.

'What about you?' Kirsten looked at him through eyes that were half-closed. She doubted whether she'd been this exhausted in her entire life.

'I'm going to go and help one of the other crews.'

'But, Joel—'

He held up his hand. 'I need to do this, Kirsten.'

'But you're exhausted.'

'I have a lot of stamina stored up and ready to burn,' he told her. 'Athletic training,' he offered by way of explanation. 'Just when you think you can't go any further, a burst of adrenalin comes on and you just take off like the wind.' He stepped forward and kissed her forehead. 'You go on back with Alex. I'm sure he'll be needing your help.'

'How will you get home?'

'There are such things as taxis,' he said with a grin. 'I'll see you in the morning.'

Kirsten placed her hands on either side of his face and kissed him—not caring who saw them. After what they'd been through tonight, what they'd shared, she felt closer to him than she had to any other man—*ever*. 'Take care,' she told him when they finally broke apart.

'I will,' he promised, before turning and heading in the direction of the other rescue teams. Kirsten turned away, her eyes misting slightly with tears. Would that be the last time she saw him? No. She brushed the thought away. Joel was a survivor. Hadn't he proved that already?

'Joel? Joel?' Kirsten was hiking through a field that was covered in knee-deep snow. 'Joel?' she called again, the falling snowflakes blurring her vision as she frantically searched for him. The snow changed to rubble and she bent to start digging with her hands. He was buried just as Frances had been, and Kirsten dug even faster.

'Wait,' she told him. 'I'll get you out. I promise.'

He closed his eyes and rested his head and Kirsten quickly checked his pulse. 'Wait,' she called again and dug harder, her hands starting to bleed. Where were her gloves? It didn't matter. She couldn't feel the pain.

'Joel?' she called again, and the word, breaking desperately from her lips, woke her. Kirsten jerked upright to find herself in her bedroom, still wearing the khaki trousers and white knit top she'd dressed in earlier that morning—yesterday morning, she mentally corrected.

She sniffed and rubbed her eyes, surprised to find them slightly damp with tears. 'Joel?' she whispered, before standing up and walking silently through the house to the door that led out to the cottage.

She peered out into the early morning and realised there was a light on in the cottage. Elation filled her heart—he was home. Then reason kicked in that perhaps he'd forgotten to switch the light off. There was only one way to find out. Quickly, Kirsten returned to her room, reached for a large woollen jumper and slipped her feet into her slippers. Without further thought, she hurried across the yard to the cottage and tapped lightly on the door.

She crossed her arms for warmth as she waited impatiently for some sort of response. 'Come on, Joel. Please, be home,' she murmured. She knocked again, a bit louder this time.

'I'm coming,' he replied, and Kirsten sighed with relief. He *was* home. When he opened the door, she had a brief moment of happiness before it was replaced by alarm. His eyes displayed his fatigue and his forehead was beaded with perspiration. She looked him over and realised that he was leaning heavily on crutches. His work trousers had been cut off above his right knee, which was firmly bandaged.

'Joel!' Concern ripped through her as she watched him manoeuvre his way to the lounge and sit down, propping his leg up on a pile of pillows. He used the crutches very well but, then, she reminded herself, he'd had a lot of practice. 'What happened?' Without waiting for an answer, she felt his forehead. 'You're burning up.' Kirsten went into the kitchen and found a towel. As she soaked it with cool water and squeezed it out, she reflected on his injury. It looked as though the Olympics wouldn't be in his immediate future after all.

When she returned she placed it on his forehead. 'Have you taken anything for the pain?' she asked in her best no-nonsense doctor's voice.

'Alex gave me an injection at the hospital. I only arrived here ten minutes ago.'

'How did you get to the cottage? You should have rung my doorbell, I could have helped you.'

'One of the paramedics was leaving the hospital and lives nearby so Alex arranged a lift for me.' Joel took Kirsten's hand in his. 'Now, stop fussing and come and sit beside me.' He was trying to lighten the mood but he didn't succeed.

'I'm not fussing,' she told him, but did as he asked. 'I'm merely concerned about you.'

'That's nice to know.' Joel closed his eyes and stroked her hand.

'I'm so glad you're back. I was worried about you.'

'I know,' he said, his voice filled with exhaustion. Kirsten tilted her head and looked at him. He was frowning again and she realised that this time it wasn't due to the pain.

'What happened?'

'We'd just moved the last patient out when a beam of wood became dislodged, swung down and hit the side of my right leg.' He shook his head, despair evident in his voice.

'What are you going to do?' she asked softly, and he opened his eyes.

'I'm going to start on my knee recovery again although, thank goodness, this injury isn't nearly as bad as my previous one.'

'What did Alex say?'

'Slight muscle and tendon damage. He X-rayed it but there was nothing out of place. He doesn't need to operate.'

'That's good news.' Kirsten was trying hard to help him find the silver lining.

'Yeah.' There was such absolute desolation in his tone that Kirsten's heart turned over with sympathy.

They were quiet for a while before she said softly, 'Joel, I'm sorry about the Olympics.'

He raised her hand to his lips and kissed it. 'Me, too.'

'I remember watching you win your silver medal. Your parents had a party and everyone stayed to cheer you on and the moment you crossed that line will live in my heart forever. It was…*glorious*.'

'Yeah.' He closed his eyes once more.

'Is that moment enough for you?' Her words were gentle, radiating support.

'I guess it will have to be.'

'Then the answer is no. Joel, if you want to get into the team, you may still have a chance. Call the physio later today and ask them to come and take a look at your knee. Ring the coach and see if you can get an extension for acceptance onto the team.'

'What about your practice?' He lifted his head and gazed into her eyes.

'I'll handle that,' she told him. 'I'll ferry you to and from any appointments. If you *need* that moment again, Joel, I'll help you in any way I can.'

'You've got Melissa coming.'

Kirsten sighed. 'I know, but if we get her involved, helping you with your leg exercises, maybe that will be good for her, too. It'll work out.'

Joel leaned forward and kissed her. 'Thank you.' There was hope in his tone. 'You're good for me, Dr Doyle.' He smiled wearily.

'I know, but you can keep on telling me,' she teased, and he laughed.

They sat like that for another ten minutes before Kirsten protested, 'I'm starting to get a cramp.' She let go of his hand and stretched, a yawn escaping as she did so. 'Let me help you get into bed.'

'Really, Dr Doyle,' he teased with that gorgeous smile

of his, and Kirsten was happy to see Joel's optimism returning.

'You know what I mean.' Kirsten helped him up and preceded him into his room, preparing the bed. She took his crutches from him as he sat down and placed them beside the bed so he'd have easy access to them when he woke. She also helped him take off his dirty shirt and trousers, calling upon the professional within to stop her from running her fingers over his perfectly sculpted chest and legs.

He was an athlete, she reminded herself. She had already admired his body through his clothes on numerous occasions during the past week, knowing that beneath those clothes his muscles would be well defined. Actually *seeing* him naked, except for a pair of satin boxer shorts, caused her heart to increase in its rhythm, the surge of blood pumping through her veins making her feel light-headed.

Kirsten plumped his pillows up with force just before he lay down, lifting his leg carefully into position. She smiled down at him. 'Have a good sleep,' she said. 'You have no plans for today so make sure you rest.'

'Yes, Doctor,' he said with a tired smile.

Kirsten sat on the edge of the bed and he took her hand in his.

'You're so good for me, Kirsten.' Within minutes, he was out for the count. Kirsten gently retrieved her hand, switched off the bedside light and walked silently through the cottage back to her own home.

Knowing he was safe had removed a huge burden from her heart, so that when she returned to bed she fell asleep instantly.

On Friday, Joel's mobile phone shrilled to life just as he was shutting the door to the cottage. He was balancing on his crutches but managed to pull the phone out and answer the call.

'Dr McElroy,' he said as he slumped into a comfortable chair.

'Hello, dear.'

'Oh, hi, Mum.' He adjusted the footstool to accommodate his leg before relaxing back.

'Is this a bad time?'

'No. I've just got home.'

'From the physio?'

'Not today. I had a hydro session this morning so thought I'd give Kirsten a hand with the house calls this afternoon. Next week the physio will be more intense so I won't be able to help her out. Oh, I've been meaning to tell you. One of the house calls we make regularly is to an elderly couple who also have six children. Fred and Doris Dawson. They're great people and Doris makes biscuits that closely rival yours.'

'Does she now? Well, perhaps I should send you some down for a proper taste test.'

'Hey, I won't say no to that. Next time you're in Canberra, I'll take you around to meet them.'

'That sounds lovely. Now, what's the report on your knee?'

'Improving every day.'

'Wonderful. I must confess that I'm glad that Jed and Jordanne are there to keep an eye on you. Don't go over-doing it, Joel.'

'I won't, Mum. I can promise you that. The Olympics mean far too much to me and the fact that I still have a chance is something I don't want to ruin.'

'But it's only been six days since you injured your knee again. Don't push it too hard.'

'I am being careful,' he said. 'Alex has cleared every-thing I'm doing.'

'Good. That makes me feel better. So now that I know how you are, tell me how Kirsten is.'

'She's fine.'

'How did she cope with the retrieval team? I know emergency medicine isn't one of her strong points,' Jane clarified.

'She was brilliant,' Joel said, unable to keep the admiration from his tone. 'I knew she was nervous but she pulled herself together and did the job that needed doing. I think the GP sessions she's doing at the hospital will definitely help her self-esteem when it comes to dealing with emergencies in the future.'

'That's good. I'm glad she did well.'

Joel heard the hint of pride in his mother's voice. 'You *really* care about her, don't you,' he stated.

'Of course,' Jane said, a little indignantly. 'I care a lot about my children's friends, and especially someone like Kirsten Doyle. I have a lot of time for her. She's always been a lovely person and I'll warn you again, Joel McElroy, that if you hurt her—'

'Mum,' he interrupted, 'I'm *not* going to hurt her.'

'Not intentionally, Joel,' Jane said, her tone immediately softening. 'You're incapable of that, but I just can't help feeling there's something…*more* going on between the two of you. Feminine intuition, a mother's love—call it what you will, but the feeling is there and I'm going with it.'

Joel breathed deeply and closed his eyes. 'You're right. There *is* something between us. Kirsten is…well, she's…'

'Starting to break through your barriers?' Jane offered.

'Yes. The way she smiles, her genuine need to help others, her perfume, her beautiful, long, hair…' He groaned and opened his eyes. 'None of that matters, though,' he said more matter-of-factly.

'Why not?'

'The Olympics, Mum. This is my last chance. Let's face

it, I'm no spring chicken when it comes to the competitive edge. The twenty-year-olds I'll be racing against have more drive and stamina than I do.'

'Oh, nonsense. If anything, it'll be your knee that weighs you down. Even a twenty-year-old would find it hard to bounce back from such an injury. You've always been a fast healer and your determination has helped tremendously over the years. You'll make the team, I have no doubt about that.'

'You're my mother. That's what you're supposed to say.'

'I disagree, dear. It's *because* I'm your mother that I can get away with the truth. My next question for you is what are you going to do *after* the Olympics?'

He shrugged. 'Probably return here. Kirsten will still need help with her practice.'

'Have you discussed this with her?'

'Not yet.'

Jane sighed deeply into the phone. 'Joel, I love you but just promise me this…' His mother's tone was caring and calm. It was a tone she used when she was about to deliver an amazing insight into a person's character. It was a gift she had and this time the person in question was himself. 'That if you feel half for Kirsten what you felt for Sylvia, then this relationship would definitely be worth pursing. I was watching the two of you at our wedding anniversary party and I noticed then that there's chemistry between the two of you. Do you remember the first time you met? It was years ago when you came home for a break between competitions.'

'No, I don't,' he whispered, and instantly wished he did but he'd been different back then. He would have simply dismissed Kirsten as another friend of his sister's.

'Kirsten had a crush on you then and her attraction has obviously intensified now which is why I've urged you to be careful if you intend playing with her heart. She's a rare

jewel, dear, and one I don't want you to lose. I understand
how important the Olympics are to you, but answer me
this…'

He waited.

'If you had the choice of winning another medal—regardless of colour—or spending the rest of your life with
your soul mate, what would you choose?'

Joel didn't answer her.

'How's Frances doing now?' Kirsten asked Jordanne the
following Thursday. It was almost two weeks since Frances
had sustained her injuries and Kirsten was keeping a close
eye on the woman she'd helped to rescue.

'Progressing slowly. Unfortunately, we've had to am-
putate two of the toes on her right foot but that's the most
drastic. We operated on her pelvis yesterday afternoon and
at this stage Alex and I are happy with the results.'

'Great. What about her femurs?'

'Both healing nicely. We put Grosse and Kempf nails
down each bone to stabilise them and they're doing the
trick. The physios are happy with her progress as well.'

'That's wonderful. How is she mentally?'

'She has a good sense of humour which is great because
it's an asset in situations such as these. She's vowing never
to take a job near snow again.' She chuckled. 'She even
refused to have ice-cubes in her water because they're cold,
just like snow.'

Kirsten smiled. 'That's good to hear.'

'And how's my brother?' Jordanne asked. 'That was the
main reason for my call,' she added.

Kirsten had just finished her morning clinic list. Usually,
she had Thursday afternoons off but as Joel was working
hard with the physiotherapist and the other locum she'd
employed had required an emergency trip to the dentist,
Kirsten was doing the afternoon clinic as well.

'Joel's coping better than I'd expected. I guess it's because of his athletic background. He seems to bounce back from injury sooner than those of us who don't exercise as strenuously.'

'He always has for as long as I can remember. If he ever cut himself, within a few days it had completely healed. As he's having physio every day, it would definitely speed up his recovery. How long has the coach given him to get his knee ready?'

'Until Christmas. The team flies out for the Winter Olympics the second week in January.'

'Do you think he'll make it?' Jordanne asked softly.

'If optimism has any say in it, yes, but you're the orthopaedic surgeon. How was he when Alex last examined him?'

'Better than Alex had hoped. It's been eleven days since his knee was injured again, and as usual Joel is making a remarkable recovery. If he keeps up this pace, I think he has a good chance of making it.'

'Some people heal faster than others,' Kirsten said wistfully.

'Are you all right?' Jordanne asked with concern.

'Yeah.'

'You don't sound too sure.'

'I've never been around anyone like Joel before. He has such…drive.' Kirsten felt a little awkward talking to Jordanne about him.

'So what's going on between you two?' Jordanne asked with her usual forthrightness.

'I wish I knew.'

'Has he kissed you yet?' Jordanne's tone radiated excitement.

Kirsten hesitated for a moment before saying, 'Yes.'

'I knew it!' her friend said triumphantly. 'So, do I say, "Welcome to the family"?'

'Ha!' Kirsten laughed ironically. 'I don't think so, Jordanne. We both have other things happening at the moment. Joel has the Olympics to train for and I have Melissa arriving at the end of the week.' She sighed. 'Nothing permanent—understand? Joel and I are just…enjoying each other's company while we can.'

'Oh, come off it,' Jordanne said a little impatiently. 'Don't try and kid me that you're the type of person who dabbles in short affairs because I know you're not. I've known you for too long, Kirsten, and you're the type of person to hang out for moonlight and magnolias. *Romance*.'

Kirsten smiled at her friend's words. It was true. She *was* a romantic at heart.

'You two are perfect for each other. Once the Olympics are over and things have settled down with Melissa, you and Joel can start your life together and live happily ever after.'

'Just like you?' Kirsten was glad she wasn't having this conversation face to face with Jordanne because there was no way she'd be able to hide the tears that had gathered in her eyes.

'Just like me,' she agreed softly.

Kirsten sniffed and laughed. 'You're a hopeless romantic, Jordanne McElroy.'

'Thank you,' Jordanne said proudly.

'I still don't know what's going to happen between us.' Kirsten's tone was dubious.

'Tell me about it,' her friend urged.

There was no hesitation this time and Kirsten was glad to finally talk to Jordanne about her feelings for Joel. 'In some ways I'm almost jealous of the time he spends working on his knee but, on the other hand, I'm determined to be positive about it. At least we've been eating dinner together most nights this week.'

'What did I tell you? Perfect for each other!'

'Yeah,' Kirsten said, her tone still a bit flat.

'Hang in there,' Jordanne encouraged. 'I know it isn't easy, believe me. When we were growing up, Joel was always off at some training session or eating a special diet or going overseas again. Don't get me wrong. I'm really proud of his accomplishments, but in some way he was my ghost brother.'

'I think I know exactly what you mean. Listen, why don't you and Alex come to dinner tomorrow night, if you're not busy? Melissa arrives on Saturday with my parents so it will be our last chance to get together for a while.'

'Sounds perfect,' Jordanne responded with enthusiasm.

'I'll call Sally and Jed and ask them, too.'

'Ooh, the six of us,' Jordanne squealed with delight. 'Let's do it. What can I bring?' They discussed the plans for the following evening before Jordanne said, 'Is that the time? Sorry, Kirsten, I have to go. We have Alex's private operating list this afternoon and he won't be a happy camper if he doesn't start on time.'

Kirsten chuckled. 'I thought you *enjoyed* getting him out of his bad moods.'

'You'd better believe it,' Jordanne said with a giggle. 'See you tomorrow.'

Kirsten tried to suppress the niggling doubt that Joel might be doing more exercises on his knee the next night, hoping that he'd manage to make it to the impromptu dinner party she'd just organised.

To take her mind off it, she threw herself into her afternoon clinic and even managed to finish early. Looking at the clock, Kirsten decided on impulse to go down to the institute to see if Joel was finished. As she grabbed her keys and bag, she also realised she *needed* to see him. She'd missed him far too much in the past few days and wanted to spend every possible moment with him.

She'd been to the institute a few times, but after five

minutes of walking up and down the row of buildings she still failed to find where the physiotherapists were located. Kirsten shook her head and headed for the library. She wished it was Friday as both Jordanne and Sally did their research here on that day, but she also remembered them talking about a librarian who knew everyone and everything about the institute.

As she pushed open the doors and walked into the library, a woman she guessed to be in her mid twenties, with blonde hair and blue eyes, looked expectantly at her.

'May I help you?'

Kirsten read the woman's name tag. 'Sky. That's right.'

'Have we met?'

'No.' Kirsten smiled. 'I'm a friend of Jordanne's and Sally's and I'm looking—'

'You must be Kirsten,' Sky interrupted.

'Yes.'

'You're looking for Joel?'

'Yes.'

'He's currently in the biodome, having some tests done. I'll check and see if he's finished.'

Before Kirsten could say another word, Sky had picked up the phone, tapped in a number and was waiting to be connected. 'Hi, sweetie,' she said into the receiver. Sky waited a moment, then giggled. 'Yeah, me, too. Listen, is Joel still there? Oh, good. Can you tell him that his girl-friend has come to pick him up?'

'But I'm not—' Kirsten said quickly as she felt her colour begin to rise. Sky waved away her words as she continued her conversation.

'Yes, of course he has a girlfriend, silly.' Sky rolled her eyes and mouthed 'men' to Kirsten. 'She's here in the library.' After a few more words to whoever was on the other end of the phone, plus a few blown kisses, Sky hung up the phone. 'He's just finished and is coming here to meet you.'

'Oh, that's not necessary. I was going to bring the car around for him.'

'That's cute,' Sky said with another laugh. 'Your hair is a gorgeous colour,' she said. Today, Kirsten had braided her hair as usual, but as she'd had a long consulting day she'd wound the braid into a bun. 'How long is it?'

'About waist-length,' Kirsten answered with a shrug.

'Wow. I'll bet that drives Joel wild.'

'How…well…do you know Joel?' Kirsten enquired.

'He usually stops by to say hello when he's here. He and Jed are so alike. Jed usually stops for a chat, too.'

'I suppose Jordanne and Sally are in here on Fridays as well?'

'Yes. I'd love to meet more of the McElroys—they seem to be a lovely family,' Sky said.

'They *are* a lovely family,' Kirsten said, her smile genuine.

'That's right. You've known them all for years, haven't you?'

'Yes,' Kirsten said, and looked up as the library doors opened.

'Hi,' Joel said with a beaming smile as he came in, leaning heavily on his walking stick. 'This is a nice surprise.' Kirsten crossed to his side. She always felt better when he was around.

'You two make a good couple,' Sky said, her eyes all dreamy. 'Take him home, Kirsten, and remember to drop in and say hello the next time you're at the institute.'

'I will,' Kirsten said, and waved goodbye.

Joel held her hand as they walked slowly to the car. Once they were seated, he leaned over to claim her lips in an electrifying kiss. Kirsten's body was overcome with desire at the way his lips gently teased and tested before he placed his hand at the back of her neck and deepened the kiss.

Kirsten raised her hand to his shirt-covered chest and caressed the hard contours beneath.

Joel broke free and looked into her eyes after they'd slowly opened. 'Do you have any idea what you do to me?' he groaned, his gaze filled with passion.

Kirsten smiled slowly and sweetly at him before nodding. 'Exactly what you do to me,' she replied, and kissed him again.

'We're never going to get home at this rate,' he said after a few more minutes.

Kirsten agreed and started the engine. She asked him how his knee was progressing and was glad that he seemed pleased with his progress.

'Hopefully I'll just have tomorrow and then I can return to a more normal pace of exercising.'

'Really?' Kirsten asked as she navigated the traffic. She hoped that would be the case. 'Your range of motion has improved that much?'

'I'd say I'm close to getting back to what it was before the skiing village rescue.'

Kirsten's smile was genuine. 'Joel, that's fantastic. Well done.'

When they arrived home, Joel helped Kirsten finish the dinner preparations before they sat down to enjoy their meal—just the two of them.

'You must be exhausted,' he said as he forked another mouthful of beef goulash into his mouth. 'This is delicious,' he commented appreciatively.

'I'm glad you like it,' she said, feeling warmed by his praise. 'It was a busy day and I'm glad it's over.'

'How are the plans for this weekend coming along?'

'Good. Dad called me earlier to say that the movers had just finish packing. They'll be sleeping there tonight before going to a hotel near the airport for tomorrow night. On Saturday morning, they fly here.'

'And Melissa? How's she coping with all of this?'

'She seems to be accepting it but she's still not talking. Mum said she's only eating one banana a day and drinking about two hundred millilitres of fluid.'

'Something is better than nothing,' he murmured and placed his hand over hers. 'Once she's settled in here, things will sort themselves out. You'll see.'

'I hope so.' Kirsten looked down at the meal she didn't feel like eating.

'Hey,' he said, and raised her chin so their eyes could meet. 'Everything will work itself out,' he promised, and leaned over to place a kiss on her lips.

Kirsten savoured the moment, breathing in deeply the scent of his aftershave. 'Mmm,' she sighed as he ended the kiss. 'I needed that.'

'Good.' He chuckled. 'Glad I could be of service.' He ate another mouthful. 'Something else is wrong, isn't it?' he guessed when she didn't brighten immediately. 'It's me,' he replied, answering his own question. 'I know we haven't seen that much of each other during the past week and a half, Kirsten, but I want you to know how much I appreciate your support. I wouldn't have been able to get this far without it. As I said, after tomorrow, which promises to be another long day, I might be able to get back to a more sedate pace of life—back to helping you out in the clinic.'

'Sounds good but there is one thing I wanted to talk to you about. I was hoping that tomorrow we could spend some time—'

'Alone?' Joel interjected, wriggling his eyebrows up and down suggestively.

'Actually, no.' She smiled. 'I've invited your siblings around with their respective spouses-to-be.'

'And you want me to get away early.' He leaned over and kissed her again. 'I'll see what I can do, but only for you.' He gave her his heart-stopping smile and Kirsten's heart thumped wildly against her ribs. She knew right then and there that she was fighting a losing battle regarding her feelings for him. She no longer needed to caution herself about falling in love with Joel because it was far too late for that. She loved him and there was nothing she could do about it!

CHAPTER SIX

ON FRIDAY, Kirsten worked her way steadily through her morning clinic before attending to the house calls. Her thoughts through the day continually turned to Joel, wondering what he was doing at that moment. Did he miss her? Did he love her as she loved him?

She checked on Fred and Doris Dawson who were sorry that Joel hadn't been able to accompany her. Nevertheless, Doris gave her some home-made biscuits to take back to him and Fred gave her a bunch of bottle-brush blossoms to 'bring some Christmas cheer' into her home. Kirsten was touched and lovingly ran her finger gently along the red blooms.

Gail Watson, the new mother of baby Patrick, was her last port of call. Kirsten had to knock twice on the door and could hear the baby crying. Eventually, a man opened the door. Kirsten recognised him as Gail's husband who had come with her for one of her antenatal check-ups.

He had a two-day growth of beard, messy hair and looked as though he hadn't slept for a week. 'Come in, Doc,' he said, and opened the door.

'Hi, Tony,' she said as she walked through and allowed him to lead her into the family room. 'Patrick still not settling?' she asked, speaking over the noise.

'No.'

The noise grew louder as Gail carried her son through the house. When she walked into the family room, she went straight to Tony and handed the screaming baby over. 'I need to have a shower,' she stated, and left as abruptly as she'd arrived.

Tony glared in the direction his wife had gone before he slumped down into the chair, Patrick still crying.

'Do you mind?' Kirsten asked, holding out her hands for the baby.

'Sure. Take him,' Tony murmured, and willingly gave his son to Kirsten. Patrick screamed even louder now that someone he didn't know was holding him. Kirsten reached into her medical bag for a torch and took the opportunity to look inside Patrick's mouth while it was open.

Next she sat down, flipped him over and peered into first one ear and then the other. She took his temperature but everything appeared normal.

'Is he *ever* quiet?' she asked Tony, who had closed his eyes and leaned his head back against the chair.

'For about two hours during the night and maybe one hour, if you're lucky, during the day.'

Kirsten looked from him back to Patrick. 'What's wrong, little man?' she asked as she stretched him out on her arm and started rubbing his back. 'Have you got some wind? Any pain?' Patrick just cried louder. 'Come on,' she crooned, 'you can tell me.' She walked up and down the room while she flicked out her mobile phone and pressed one of the pre-set numbers.

'Hello, June? It's Kirsten.'

'It sounds as though you're at the Watson household,' the midwife replied.

Kirsten smiled. 'Gee, I wonder how you guessed. Listen, are you free at the moment?'

'Yes. I think we should get this baby sorted out once and for all before his parents drop from complete exhaustion.'

'Thanks.' Kirsten ended the call, and when she looked across at Tony his eyes were still closed, his mouth was open and he was snoring. 'It looks as though it's you and me, Patrick,' she told him. She continued pacing up and down, trying him in different positions. Eventually, after fifteen minutes or so, his cries slowly subsided before stopping. She peered at him but he wasn't asleep. 'At least you're quiet,' she said, feeling the beginnings of a headache coming on.

Kirsten heard a car pull up outside and crossed to the door just as Gail came back into the room, looking refreshed from her shower. She took one look at her husband, sound asleep on the couch and snorted, saying, 'Typical.'

She went to take Patrick back from Kirsten. 'Actually, I think June's here so would you mind answering the door?'

Gail turned sharply on her heel and crossed to the door. She waited until the midwife came in before returning to Kirsten, her hands open. 'I'll take him. He's my son,' she snapped, and this time Kirsten handed Patrick over. Thankfully, the little one decided not to scream his lungs out and snuggled contentedly into his mother before closing his eyes and drifting off to sleep.

Gail looked from Kirsten to June before raising her chin defiantly. 'You don't think I can cope, do you?' she asked, her tone accusing.

'That's not it at all,' Kirsten replied.

'Why don't I make us all a cup of tea?' June suggested, and went into the kitchen. Kirsten knew both she and June would have to be careful if they were to help Gail and Tony at all. From the symptoms Gail was exhibiting, it appeared she was suffering from postnatal depression.

Gail woke her husband up and together the four of them—or, more correctly, the five of them, including Patrick—sat down to discuss the matter.

'I want you both to know that June and I are here to help you. Regardless of what you might think, we're not accusing anyone. In fact, no one should be blamed because that won't do either of you any good.' Kirsten looked from one to the other and noticed the glares they were giving each other.

'What we need to focus on here is getting both of you back to your normal selves. Sleep deprivation won't help either. The best way you can be effective parents for Patrick is to make sure you're getting enough sleep.'

'I'm coping just fine,' Gail said.

'That's a laugh,' Tony interjected.

'What's that supposed to mean?' Gail snipped back.

'You are *not* coping, Gail.'

'I most certainly am. *You're* the one who isn't coping,' she returned.

'That's enough!' June said firmly, silencing both of them. 'If you keep this up, you'll wake Patrick again.'

Both parents turned their eyes to Patrick who was still snuggled into the crook of Gail's arm. 'Just as well I'm holding the baby,' she said, and glared at her husband again.

'So why don't you put him down?'

'You know why. He wakes up. Gosh, Tony, you've been home for the past four weeks and you still don't know his routine.'

'He hasn't got one,' Tony retorted. 'My mother has offered to come around and help but, no, you're too proud to take her help.'

'Her *help*, as you call it, is to put me down, make me feel like a moron and then tell me that Patrick is fine screaming his lungs out and that he'll eventually cry himself to sleep!' Gail's voice began to rise and when Patrick started to whimper she quickly started rocking from side to side, patting his bottom.

Kirsten spoke softly. 'Gail, you're a very good mother. Despite what anyone else might say, you love your son and that's evident in the way you're holding him right now. Tony, you, too, love your son and I'll tell you how I know.

There's not one single sign of neglect. Patrick is fed, he's wearing clean clothes, his nappy is changed regularly and the way that you both hold him tenderly, as though he were a piece of china that might break, indicate that you are wonderful parents.'

'What you *are* both suffering from is sleep deprivation,' June added.

'That's right,' Kirsten continued. 'A lot of first-time parents are often shocked at the amount of work required when a new baby comes home. It seems so easy in hospital, with midwives there to help you, and you're sure you can cope. Slowly but steadily you start to go downhill, especially when you're not getting much sleep. One or two nights you can cope with, but this has been going on for four weeks now.'

'We'd like you *all* to consider going to the Queen Elizabeth II family hospital or, as we call it, the QE II. This is a hospital *specifically* designed for parents and babies. There are also women in there who haven't had their babies yet and require specialised treatment.'

'I don't need to go,' Gail denied.

'Honey,' Tony said, and touched her shoulder, 'will you listen to them? I for one could use a good night's sleep. I've only got one more week off from work and I don't want you to be at home by yourself with Patrick screaming all day. This baby was supposed to make us happy.'

'I need to think about it,' Gail said finally, and Kirsten smiled.

'Good. That's all we're asking at this stage.'

She and June stayed to help out with some of the household chores before Kirsten left the midwife to help Gail, even though Gail insisted she didn't need any help, through Patrick's evening bath and feed.

As Kirsten climbed into her car, she glanced at the time. 'Oh, good heavens. Everyone will be arriving within half

Sally washed and dried her hands then embraced Kirsten. 'These things have a way of working themselves out,' she encouraged. 'You and Joel are at the very beginning of a relationship, but trust me when I say that he *will* outgrow the need for professional competition. I was a professional athlete once. I won gold but even if I hadn't won anything, the desire to be the best of the best does wane. Joel will find something in life that will give him the same sort of…buzz, I'd guess you'd call it, and when he realises what that is, he won't need to compete professionally any more. For me it was medicine, and I'm really happy with my choice. After all, if I wasn't a doctor, I would never have met you or Jordanne and I certainly would never have met Jed.' At the mention of her fiancé, Sally's eyes misted over with love.

'I hope you're right, Sally.'

'If you want a second opinion, why not talk to Jane McElroy? The woman has the most amazing insights.'

'I don't know if I'd feel comfortable talking to her about her own son.'

'Why not? She's the best person to ask. I found her insights regarding Jed were very accurate.'

'I'll think about it,' Kirsten replied, still a little dazed with the prospect of talking to Joel's mother about him. It was true that Kirsten had the highest respect in the world for Jane McElroy, especially as she had been like a second mother to her during those long and seemingly endless med school years.

Jordanne and Alex arrived right on time and Jed and Joel weren't far behind them. Kirsten was very conscious that this was the first time her friends had seen her with Joel and she accepted his kiss with slight embarrassment.

Jordanne, being the effervescent person that she was, threw her arms around both of them in delight.

Dinner was a relaxed and easygoing affair and, thanks

to Sally's help in preparing the meal, everything was ready right on time. The topics they discussed ranged from the latest medical breakthroughs, the price of postage stamps and, of course, Jed's and Sally's upcoming wedding.

'It's five weeks tomorrow to the big day,' Jed announced as he finished his dessert and placed his arm around Sally.

'Will you be away for Christmas?' Alex asked.

'We're going away to the Blue Mountains for a week, then returning for the McElroys' annual tree-trimming party on Christmas Eve,' Sally replied. 'I must confess that I'm really looking forward to this Christmas.' There was excitement in her words and expression, and Kirsten felt a wave of happiness for her friend.

'Your first *real* Christmas with your family—*all* of your family,' Jordanne said. 'I'm so happy for you, Sally.'

Sally's father, Norman Bransford, was a very rich businessman and had treated his only child as a commodity rather than a person until just a few months ago when he'd sustained a terrible, life-threatening injury. Jed had been first on the scene and had resuscitated Norman when he'd stopped breathing. Jordanne and Alex had been the surgeons to operate on him and the whole incident had made Sally's father realise his previous mistakes and the importance of family.

Kirsten served the coffee and tea in the lounge room, accompanied by the home-made biscuits Doris had sent for Joel.

'Looks as though you have an admirer,' Jed teased his brother.

'An admirer who makes delicious biscuits—gee, that's a hard one to cope with,' Joel joked, and Kirsten smiled at him. He really did enjoy seeing patients and getting to know them. He was a people person, she realised, and it was this quality that made him a good doctor as well as a good skier. The happiness waned for a second as the thought of him leaving for the Olympics passed through her mind, but she brushed it aside.

It was close to midnight when they finally left and she slumped down into the soft lounge cushions, happy and exhausted. Joel sat down beside her.

'You did an incredible job,' he murmured as his arms encircled her. He drew her close to his side and Kirsten rested her head on his shoulder. 'You're a born hostess,' he remarked, his hand stroking her hair.

They stayed where they were for a few minutes before the scent of his aftershave began teasing at her senses. Kirsten sat up and took the band out of her hair, loosening the braid so her auburn locks cascaded down her back.

'I love it when you do that,' Joel whispered, his voice thick with emotion. Kirsten smiled sensually.

'I know,' she replied, and leaned across to kiss him. Joel's hands plunged into her hair, gathering handfuls and holding her head firmly near his, ensuring that she didn't pull away. He needn't have worried, though, for she wasn't going anywhere. She put her heart and soul into the kiss, letting him know with actions and emotions the extent of her feelings for him.

She worked the buttons on his shirt undone, her fingers clumsily fumbling, while her mouth never once left his. When she had the top three buttons undone, she pushed the material impatiently aside and started trailing hot kisses down his chin, across his neck and onto his chest.

Joel groaned, his fingers still trailing gently through her hair. Kirsten's kisses started heading up again and when she reached his earlobe she nibbled gently at it, enjoying the shudder that ripped through him.

He tugged lightly on her hair, urging her mouth around to meet his own, and this time when their lips met it was with a force so mind-blowing that Kirsten wondered whether she'd ever recover. She loved him, with all her heart, soul and mind. She belonged in his arms—for ever.

'You're…a…very…desirable…woman,' he murmured. Each word was punctuated by a kiss and Kirsten was pleased to note that his breathing was as ragged as her own. Joel gazed into her eyes and she knew he could see his own desire and passion reflected in their green depths. He kissed her at a more leisurely pace before holding her head close to his chest.

As their breathing slowly returned to normal, Kirsten enjoyed listening to his heart beating its steady rhythm. Joel stroked her hair and they were simply content to hold each other for the next ten minutes. Although, as they did, she became aware of Joel withdrawing from her, perhaps not physically but definitely mentally.

'I'd better go,' he said as he slowly eased away from her. Kirsten looked at him and he must have read the confusion in her eyes. 'There's nothing wrong,' he said as he stood and reached for his walking stick.

'Then what is it? Please, tell me.' He was silent for so long that Kirsten drew her own conclusions as to what, or rather *who*, had come between them. 'Are you thinking about Sylvia?' she asked softly, not sure whether she wanted to know the answer.

Joel nodded once.

'I see.' Kirsten crossed her arms over her body and looked down in despair.

'It's not what you think,' he said urgently, and she looked up at him.

'Then tell me. Are we similar? Do I remind you of her?'

'No. If anything, you're practically opposite—in looks, in personality.'

'Does that bother you?'

'Kirsten…' Joel said and sat down beside her again, taking one of her hands in his. He took a deep breath. 'I'm not the same man I was when Sylvia died. I've changed so much I hardly recognise myself some days.'

'Tell me,' she pleaded quietly.

He looked into her eyes but she could tell he wasn't seeing her. He was remembering.

'I was wild back then. I lived to ski and I was a bit of a rebel. The year I won silver I was almost kicked off the team because I'd disobeyed the coach's orders. That was the year I met Sylvia and she was a real dare-devil—the woman had no fear. She was a member of the Swiss ski team and when we got together...' Joel shook his head in disbelief. 'I'm amazed that we weren't both killed with some of the risks we took. No mountain was too high, no slope too steep.' He paused and took a deep breath.

'She was always looking for a new thrill—searching for a challenge to make the adrenaline rush last longer. The night she died, we'd been doing just that—searching for the thrill—and we'd found it. We listened to the weather forecast before we left so we knew what might happen. Sylvia said it was part of the experience. Even when I tried to say no to her, she talked me round.' Joel shook his head. 'If only I'd stopped her.'

Kirsten reached out and touched his face in sympathy. She hated to see him still hurting.

'I couldn't save her,' he whispered, his voice choked with disgust. 'I didn't have the medical skills or the equipment, but that's still no excuse. If I'd been more forceful with her, spoken my mind. Kept saying no—'

'She'd probably have gone without you,' Kirsten interrupted. 'Joel, her death wasn't your fault.'

'I know that,' he said, and kissed her hand. 'I've worked through my guilt and despair but I still feel angry with myself for not standing up to what I knew was wrong. My parents had always taught us that. I just wish I'd applied it.'

'We all make mistakes, Joel, and you've obviously learnt from yours. You yourself have realised that you're not the man you used to be.'

'I'm not,' he said quietly as he drew her close. 'You smell of sugar and spice and all things nice,' he murmured, then his lips found hers once more.

This time the kiss they shared was very possessive, as though they were desperate to put their 'mark' on each other. Joel held her close, as close to his body as he could possibly get without hurting his knee, and Kirsten loved every minute of it.

Kirsten pulled away first. 'Oxygen,' she panted. 'We both need it.' She gazed up at him, her eyes filled with a dreamy contentment, and smiled.

Joel kissed her eyes closed and briefly brushed his lips against hers once more. 'I have to go.' His voice was thick with desire and regret. 'As much as I'd love to stay, I have exercises to do before bed and both of us have a busy day tomorrow.'

Kirsten nodded. 'Yes, we do.'

Joel laced his fingers with hers and together they walked to the door. 'Sleep sweet, Kirsten,' he said with a smile that shot straight to her heart, before claiming her lips again.

As Kirsten watched him walk across the back yard and enter the cottage, she pressed her hand to the door. 'I love you, Joel,' she sighed hopelessly.

CHAPTER SEVEN

KIRSTEN was shocked when she saw Melissa. She was holding on to her grandmother's hand as they disembarked from the plane and entered the arrivals lounge. The girl had lost weight and her face was drawn and sunken, her blonde hair hanging limply by her face. Dark circles beneath her blue eyes made Kirsten want to weep for the child who was struggling to come to terms with her parents' death.

Instead, she forced the emotions back and pasted on a large smile. 'Hello, Lissy,' she said softly, using the nickname Melissa had allowed only her the privilege of using, before scooping the girl up into a hug. To her surprise, Melissa wound her arms about Kirsten's neck and squeezed tightly. Perhaps she had been wrong to return to Canberra after the funeral without Melissa, but both she and her parents had thought it necessary for Melissa to keep seeing the grief counsellor at the Children's Hospital in Sydney.

Melissa started crying and buried her face into Kirsten's shoulder. 'Shh, darling,' Kirsten whispered, trying desperately to hold on to her own tears. 'Everything will be fine.' She kissed Melissa's head and tried to wipe away the tears, but it appeared Melissa had decided to hibernate on Kirsten's shoulder. 'Hi, Mum, Dad.' She kissed her parents who both had looks of relief on their faces.

When she'd spoken to her mother the previous night, Isobelle had said, 'Hopefully, now that we'll all be in Canberra together, the darling girl can have some sense of family—of belonging again.'

The drive from the airport was achieved with Greg Doyle driving Kirsten's car while she sat in the back close to

115

Melissa who had refused to let her go. When they arrived at her home, again the four-year-old clung to Kirsten as though she were a lifeline—which she guessed she probably was.

Not wanting to overwhelm the child, she carried her around the house, showing her each room, and when Melissa saw the room that was to be hers, with her bed and all her toys in it, she wriggled down from Kirsten's arms and ran to the other end of the house, hiding beneath the computer desk.

'I thought I was doing the right thing,' Kirsten said to Isobelle, completely bewildered by the child's attitude. 'I thought she'd be happy to see those familiar things.'

'Maybe it brings back memories she doesn't want to remember,' Isobelle said, and kissed her daughter's cheek.

'Great. That's another mistake I've made.'

'You can't expect miracles straight away, dear,' her mother soothed. 'She needs time.'

Kirsten tried to coax Melissa out but the child refused to even look at her. Eventually she gave up but not before telling the little girl just how much she loved her.

'I think I'll just head three houses up to our new home and see if the movers have arrived yet,' Greg said.

'I thought they weren't due until midday,' Kirsten said and glanced at the clock. 'Is it that time *already*?'

Greg smiled at Kirsten. 'You'll find time just slips away now that Melissa's here.'

Isobelle laughed. 'Children are the biggest and best ways to waste your time. They're so precious.'

'That sounds like something *my* mother would say,' a deep male voice said from the doorway.

They all turned to see Joel standing there, dressed casually in a pair of navy shorts and a white polo shirt, his knee firmly strapped. He came into the room, still leaning heavily on his walking stick.

'You must be Joel,' Isobelle said, and stood to embrace him. 'From the things your mother has told me about you, I feel as though I know you already,' she said. Greg and Joel shook hands.

Kirsten's heart swelled with love as he walked into the room and her knees weakened when he smiled at her. Her pulse rate increased and she suddenly found she was short of breath. Her lips parted and she smiled shyly at him, unsure what to do next.

She'd had a very emotional morning, so far, and with Joel's unannounced presence she wasn't sure whether to kiss him or pretend there was nothing going on between them. She hadn't got around to telling her parents about her burgeoning relationship with Joel because every time they'd spoken they'd discussed Melissa.

Joel, however, took the matter out of her hands by coming across and giving her a quick peck on the cheek. 'How are you holding up?' he asked softly, and touched her shoulder in concern. Kirsten looked deeply into those mesmerising blue eyes of his, drawing strength from his nearness.

She took a breath and shook her head. 'Not too good, I'm afraid. Melissa took one look at her new room and hid under my computer desk.'

Joel nodded. 'She'll come out when she's ready. Jasmine's four-year-old does the same thing.'

'Yes but Jasmine's four-year-old hasn't lost both of her parents,' Kirsten pointed out quietly. She rubbed her fingers across her forehead and sighed.

'True, but if you're that worried about her, I'll get her out,' he volunteered with a nonchalant shrug.

Kirsten's frowned deepened. 'How?'

'Ah.' He waggled his finger at her and smiled his devastating smile. 'Wait and see.'

'As much as I'd like to stick around for the show, I'll

go and check on those movers,' Greg said, and headed out the back door.

'May I have a piece of paper and a pencil, please?' Joel placed his walking stick on the chair. Kirsten handed him the materials and watched him walk, the professional within her impressed at his range of movement while the woman within appreciated the firm muscled thighs and the curve of his butt. He disappeared into the room where Melissa was hiding and Kirsten started to follow him.

She felt her mother's hand on her arm, stopping her. 'Give him a minute, dear.' She looked at her daughter, her green eyes curious. 'Not that I want to pry, but how long have you and Joel been seeing each other?'

'Well, we're kind of…just starting…' Kirsten stopped, blushing a little.

'I see.' Isobelle smiled softly but there was hesitation in her voice.

'What? You don't approve?' Kirsten asked, surprised.

'That's not it, dear.' Isobelle started to speak then hesitated before continuing, 'You'll be making a lot of adjustments in the next few months, darling, and it's bound to put a strain on any new relationships you might have formed.' Isobelle patted Kirsten's arm. 'Just be careful.'

'I will,' Kirsten promised. She kissed her mother's cheek before heading towards the study. She wasn't sure what she had expected to find but she *was* surprised to see Melissa partially out of her hiding spot, watching intently to see what Joel was drawing on the paper.

He was lounging on the floor, his injured leg straight, the other bent. 'Want to have a turn?' he asked, and put the pencil down. 'You can do it, I know you can,' he encouraged softly, and Kirsten's heart turned over with love at his compassion towards her niece.

Melissa seemed to shrink backwards but Joel ignored it and turned to look over his shoulder. 'Hi.' He smiled brightly at Kirsten and patted the carpet next to him. 'Come and sit down.'

Kirsten walked into the room, her gaze darting from Joel to Melissa and back again. She smiled and did as he'd asked. 'What are you drawing?'

'Ah, it's a surprise,' he told her, and tapped the side of his nose knowingly. 'Isn't it, Melissa?' he asked rhetorically. 'Oh, Kirsten, can you help me to remember to ask Doris Dawson for her biscuit recipe the next time we're there? I keep forgetting. You see, I told my mother about Doris's fabulous biscuits and now she wants the recipe.'

Kirsten frowned at him, wondering why he was bringing this up now. 'Sure,' she replied, and was about to say more when she saw something move out of the corner of her eye. She glanced across. It was the pencil. Melissa had picked up the pencil!

Kirsten couldn't believe it. Even though the child hadn't said a word, she was communicating. She breathed in deeply, elation filling her lungs.

'Not that my mum makes awful biscuits,' he said with a hint of impatience in his tone which caused her to shift her gaze quickly to him. 'Quite the opposite. It's just that Doris's biscuits are so delicious I'm sure my dad would appreciate a taste,' he continued without changing his tone.

Dawning realisation hit Kirsten with full force. 'Oh. Oh, of course. Yes, good idea.' She nodded for emphasis, her gaze darting surreptitiously to see what Melissa was doing while she and Joel continued with inconsequential and irrelevant chatter.

After a minute or so, Melissa put the pencil down and crawled back beneath the desk. Joel simply finished what he was saying and turned very casually to look at the paper.

'What?' He frowned down at the page. 'How did *that* happen?' His tone was one of teasing disbelief.

'What is it?' Kirsten asked, feigning curiosity.

'Something very…strange…' he drawled the word '…has happened. I drew this picture of a silly old bear and now there's two of them.'

'That *is* very strange,' Kirsten said. She glanced at Melissa who was hiding her mouth behind her hands, her eyes twinkling with mischief. A gasp of pure delight caught in Kirsten's throat at the sight, but she quickly covered up by clearing her throat. 'Maybe your hand drew another picture when you weren't looking?' she asked Joel.

He thought about this for a moment and nodded slowly. 'You might be right, Kirsten. What a funny hand I have.'

Melissa pulled her hands away from her mouth, which had curved up into a smile, and scrambled out from beneath the desk. She raced out of the room and Kirsten looked at Joel in alarm.

'What happened? I thought everything was going fine.' She started to get to her feet but he reached out a hand to stop her.

'Just wait,' he soothed her patiently, caressing her hand in his, causing a flood of tingles to spread throughout her body. 'When she comes back, keep talking like we were.'

Kirsten nodded, and when they heard footsteps heading their way Joel dropped her hand and started talking about an article he'd read in a journal.

Moments later Melissa burst into the study, holding something behind her back. Joel broke off from what he was saying to Kirsten and looked at her. 'Hello,' he said with a smile, and when Melissa brought a small yellow bear out from behind her back, Kirsten's jaw dropped open in amazement.

Not only had Joel managed to get her out from beneath the computer desk, he'd made Melissa communicate *and* go into her new room. Tears misted her eyes but for the first time in weeks they were tears of complete happiness.

'Wow! A bear! Just like we drew in our pictures,' Joel

exclaimed, and held out his hand for the toy Melissa offered. 'He's great. Isn't he, Kirsten?'

'Great,' she repeated with a big smile, and held out her
arms to Melissa. The action was completely impulsive and
the instant she'd done it Kirsten wondered whether it was
another mistake. Melissa hesitated for a split second before
rushing to her and burying her face in Kirsten's shoulder
again, but this time she was smiling shyly.

Kirsten breathed in deeply, feeling that she might be able
to cope after all. Especially if Joel was around. He was
amazing. She wanted to kiss him senseless in appreciation
but decided it would have to wait until later.

'You're a magician,' she said softly.

He shook his head and slowly heaved himself off the
floor. 'Not a magician. Parenting is all about trial and er-
ror.'

'And since when have *you* been a parent?' she chided
softly as she also stood.

Joel smiled at both of them. 'Uncle, parent. Close enough
some days,' he said with a shrug, before heading out of the
room.

He spent the rest of the day with them, acting as a buffer
for the new relationship between Kirsten and Melissa. Both
girls were happy when he was around and Kirsten knew
she wouldn't be able to thank him enough for his help and
support. It was more than she'd ever expected from him
but perhaps she'd been wrong to underestimate him. In her
previous experiences with the opposite sex, not many men
would have wanted to know her now she was a single parent. Yet here was Joel, pitching in and helping out.

He stayed for dinner and Melissa's bath, tickling the
child when she was wrapped up in a bright yellow fluffy
towel.

'Is yellow your favourite colour?' he asked softly, and
Melissa gave the slightest nod.

Kirsten shook her head again in disbelief. Joel had accomplished more with Melissa in one afternoon than the grief counsellor had done in several weeks. Then, again, maybe it was the grief counsellor's work that was paying off. Either way, Kirsten felt a sense of hope that everything would turn out right in the end.

That was until Joel left and it was time for Melissa to go to bed. She turned on the tears and threw a tantrum. Kirsten had never seen anyone so stubborn—except for Jacqui, Melissa's mother.

'Come on, sweetie,' Kirsten pleaded as she took a disposable nappy from the pack her mother had left. They were more like pants, specifically designed with elastic edges, making them easier to pull up and down.

Poor Melissa had started wetting the bed again but, as her mother had informed her, the grief counsellor had assured them that it was a normal occurrence in these sorts of circumstances.

'Come here, Lissy, and put your nightie on. Look, it's got your favourite yellow bear on it,' she said, holding the nightie up. Melissa refused and started crying again. Kirsten groaned, feeling totally exhausted and drained.

'Come on, Lissy, my love.' She picked the child up and sat down on the lounge. Reaching for the remote control, she switched the television on and cuddled the little girl who eventually stopped crying. Soon her breathing was deep and relaxed as she drifted off to sleep. Kirsten watched a bit more of a programme before her own eyes started to droop. She really should get up off the lounge and head for bed, but every muscle in her body ached, making her doubt she had the strength to move.

Besides, she'd wanted to watch this programme…

Kirsten jerked her head upright and looked around the room. The lights were still on. The television screen showed the Australian flag, flying from Parliament House, and the national anthem was being played.

Kirsten squinted at the clock. Surely it wasn't *that* late. When the anthem finished, the test pattern came up, indicating the television station had shut down for the evening. She looked down at the sleeping child who had snuggled into the crook of her arm.

'I think we should both get to bed,' she whispered, and tried to stand. It was impossible. Melissa was a dead weight in her arms, but at least that meant she was getting good REM sleep.

Kirsten wriggled and shifted, slowly moving forward so she could stand. As she did so, she realised her legs felt wet. She whimpered in defeat as she realised she hadn't put a disposable nappy on Melissa. Now they were both wet.

She thought for a moment before deciding how best to tackle the problem. Still cradling the girl in her arms, she went to the linen closet and grabbed a towel, pulling a few down to the ground with it.

'I'll pick you up later,' she told them. Next, she struggled to spread the towel out on Melissa's bed, nearly dropping the child twice. Finally she was able to gently transfer her across. The instant the weight was gone, she gave her arms a good shake to restore the blood circulation.

Thank goodness Melissa had remained asleep. Kirsten quickly went to the bathroom, putting the towels back in the cupboard on the way, and fixed herself up. After she'd cleaned her teeth, she returned to Melissa's room, changed her clothes, put the nappy on and managed to get the nightie over her head. The child slept on.

'Better,' she announced, proud of herself. Yet the instant Kirsten was tucked up in her own bed, a strangled scream came from Melissa's room.

'Mummy! Mummy!' she yelled. 'Mummy.'

Kirsten's heart hammered against her ribs at the distressing sound. She tumbled out of bed, catching her foot in the covers and falling to the ground, hitting her leg on the bedside table. 'Ouch,' she whimpered as she hobbled down the corridor.

'Shh, darling,' she said on entering Melissa's room. The girl was sitting up in bed, tears streaming down her face, her eyes closed in sleep.

'Mummy!' she called again, her voice laced with anguish.

'It's all right, Lissy. I'm here,' Kirsten whispered soothingly as she enveloped the child in her arms. 'It's all right,' she said again as Melissa clung to her. 'Shh, darling.' Kirsten rocked the child from side to side, brushing the blonde hair from her eyes and kissing her head.

The sobs tore at the little body and Kirsten joined in, wondering how on earth she was going to help this child cope with her grief.

Eventually they both quietened and Kirsten leaned back against the pillow, still holding Melissa firmly in her arms. 'Shh, darling,' she said and kissed her head. 'We'll get there.'

'So, how are things going?' Jordanne asked the following Friday.

Kirsten held the phone between her ear and shoulder as she finished typing up her last patient's notes. 'I'm exhausted,' she said. 'Not one night since Melissa arrived have I had a good night's sleep.'

Jordanne chuckled. 'You sound like my sister. Welcome to the world of parenting.' She sobered before asking, 'Has Melissa spoken yet?'

'The only time I've heard her talk is when she's having nightmares, and I'd hardly call it talking,' Kirsten replied, recalling the countless times she'd woken to the child screaming in anguish. 'She has started nodding yes and no, so that's a good sign. Either I sleep in her bed or she sleeps in mine. I have a permanent crick in my neck and my back aches. I know it's probably wrong to encourage her to sleep with me, but at the moment, Jordanne, I'll do *anything* for a good night's sleep.'

'Fair enough,' Jordanne replied, and hesitated slightly before asking, 'How about you and Joel? Have you seen him much now that he's not so heavily involved in his physiotherapy? Has absence made the heart grow fonder?'

'Jordanne, you *are* a hopeless romantic,' Kirsten replied. 'He came over on Saturday afternoon when Melissa arrived and was incredible with her.'

'He's always been good with kids. My nieces and nephews love it when Uncle Joel is home. He spends a lot of time with them and is friendly but firm—just like our dad. He'll make a terrific father some day.'

'Hmm,' Kirsten replied, not wanting to say anything that might commit her in the future. She'd often thought, watching him with Melissa, how wonderful he'd be with children of his own—*their* children. The thought had brought a warm tinge to her cheeks every time and now was no exception. They'd have auburn-haired children with the same deep blue eyes as all the McElroy children and grandchildren had. 'Hmm,' Kirsten said again and focused her attention back on the conversation at hand.

'He's been over every night this week, but it's mainly been to have dinner and spend some time playing with Melissa.' Kirsten tried to keep her tone light. As far as she and Joel spending time together—alone—it was basically non-existent. Then again, what had she expected with a grieving child in the house?

'Does it bother you?' her friend asked carefully, and Kirsten felt the control on her emotions break.

'Of course it bothers me,' Kirsten snapped, then quickly

apologised. 'I'm sorry, Jordanne.' She sighed heavily. 'There's not a lot I can do about our relationship at this stage. Melissa has to be my top priority,' she said, realising that soon Joel would be getting ready to head off overseas for his attempt at Olympic gold. 'I'm sure Joel understands.'

'Oh, he'd understand, all right,' Jordanne reflected. 'Priorities have always been important to him. I guess they'd have to be to a professional athlete. You need to be completely focused on what you're doing, with no outside distractions. It can be hard to accept, especially if *you're* the distraction.'

'Hmm,' Kirsten answered again.

'So, how's the new locum settling in?' Jordanne asked, and Kirsten was thankful that her friend had tactfully changed the subject.

'Extremely well. He does most of the afternoon sessions, which leaves me free to either do my house calls or spend time with Melissa.'

'How is she handling you going to work?'

'All right,' Kirsten replied slowly. 'Monday was difficult because she cried when I left her at my parents' place. It's not that she doesn't love them—she does. They're the only grandparents she's ever known, but...' She trailed off and sighed. 'I just want to wrap her up in cotton wool and kiss away the pain.'

'But you can't,' Jordanne agreed.

'I've enrolled her into a playgroup on Thursday afternoons so she can mix with other kids her age. I'll be staying with her so it will be good for us to have that time together. At least, I hope so. I'm at the stage where I'll try anything if it's going to work.'

'Sounds like a good idea. Do you start next week?'

'Yes,' Kirsten said as someone knocked at her door. 'Come in,' she called, the smile on her face blossoming and her heart increasing its usual regular rhythm when Joel walked into the room. 'Your brother has just walked in,' she said, and attempted to clear the instant huskiness from her tone. 'I'd better go.'

'Hey, don't let me stop you two spending a few precious moments together. Go get him,' Jordanne said, then promptly hung up.

Kirsten did the same and watched as Joel crossed the room, coming to stand beside her. She closed her eyes and breathed deeply when he put his hands on her shoulders, massaging away some of the tension. 'Mmm,' she groaned, her breathing beginning to settle down.

'I'm taking you out to dinner tonight,' he told her firmly.

Kirsten tensed immediately. 'I can't, Joel. I don't have the luxury of doing what I want any more. You know that. I have to go home to Melissa.'

'I'm sure your parents won't mind having her for a few extra hours.'

'It's not fair on Melissa,' she pointed out, and shrugged out from beneath his hands. She stood and faced him. 'She would have been there all day. I don't want her to feel that I'm abandoning her again.'

'When did you abandon her?' he asked, his brow furrowing into a frown.

Kirsten looked at him, regret in her eyes. 'After the funeral. I stayed for a few days and then I came back here to Canberra. I should have just brought her with me then and sorted everything else out later.'

'I thought the grief counsellor advised that she stay with your parents?'

'He did but that doesn't mean he was right. Oh, look, I'm not knocking the guy. I'm sure he's very intuitive in the area of grief-stricken children.' Kirsten pressed her fingers to her temple. 'All I'm saying is that perhaps it was the wrong thing to do. Not long after her parents die, I up and leave for Canberra.'

'I thought she loved being with your parents?'

'She does but as Jacqui was a year younger than me, I'm more a mother figure, which is obviously what she's needed.' And *you* as a father figure, Kirsten added silently. 'You've seen her this week. She's slowly been eating more, and although she's still not sleeping well…' Kirsten rubbed her lower back '…she *is* improving.'

'And that's a credit to you. I'm not asking you to go away for the weekend,' he said softly as he placed his hands back on her shoulders and looked down into her eyes. 'I only think you should get away from everything for a few hours—purely for *your* sake. Recharge your batteries. Kirsten, you've been thrown in at the deep end with Melissa. Most parents begin with a baby so that by the time the child is four years old they have a fair idea of how to cope.'

'What is that supposed to mean?' she asked as she jerked away from his touch, her chin raised defiantly. She was physically tired and mentally drained. His suggestion made sense but she felt it was too soon to leave Melissa with her parents for any longer than was necessary. Now it seemed as though he was criticising her.

'It means that coping with children is difficult,' he pointed out softly, not rising to the annoyance in her tone. 'I'm merely stating a fact. I've watched how my siblings cope with their families. I saw first-hand how my parents raised the six of us. I'm not criticising you, I'm merely pointing out a fact. It is difficult to raise a child—especially on your own.'

'But I'm not on my own,' she pointed out. 'I have my parents to help me. That's why they moved to Canberra.'

'Exactly,' he said with a hint of triumph. 'They're here to help *you*.'

'That still doesn't mean I want to leave Melissa there tonight.' Kirsten drew a deep breath and exhaled. When Joel opened his arms to her, she didn't hesitate to take advantage of them.

As she stood there, her head leaning against his chest, she felt herself begin to crumble. 'I just want to do what's right for Melissa, Joel, but half the time I have no idea what that is!'

His arms tightened about her and he kissed the top of her head. 'I know. I know, but I also know that we're *all* here to help you. Sally might not have had experience with siblings or being an aunty but the rest of us have. Well,' he added with a hint of humour, 'Jed, Alex and myself have had experience in being uncles—not aunties—but you know what I mean.'

Kirsten found herself smiling and she pulled back to look up at him. 'Thank you,' she whispered, and kissed him. 'I know you're all willing to help but there are some things we'll have to work through—just Melissa and myself.'

'I agree,' he said, and returned her kiss.

Kirsten gave herself up to the moment and allowed the gentle touch of his mouth on hers to relax her body. He was just what she needed—a 'fix' of Joel. She sighed into the embrace and revelled in the way he made her feel—all tingly and giddy and cared for. His fingers gently massaged the lower part of her spine and a groan escaped from her lips.

'That's the spot,' she murmured when she broke free.

'Is Melissa still sleeping in your bed?' he asked.

Her eyes snapped open and she frowned at him. She hadn't mentioned anything about the musical beds she'd been playing with her niece all week long. 'How—'

'I know about these things, remember,' he interrupted, and kissed her briefly once more before urging her head back to his chest. Kirsten sighed again and allowed herself to emotionally lean on him. 'How about this idea, then? If you don't like the idea of just the two of us going out, why don't we take Melissa with us?'

'What?' She pulled back to look into his deep blue eyes—eyes that were smiling with triumph. 'Out to dinner?'

A deep laugh rumbled in his chest and Kirsten delighted at the sound. 'It has been done before,' he replied, and kissed the tip of her nose.

'But…but *where*?'

'Kirsten, there are a lot of child-friendly restaurants around.'

'I don't really feel like a hamburger for dinner,' she said, screwing her nose up.

'That's not what I meant. Listen, I'll take care of the arrangements for dinner and both you and Melissa can simply relax and enjoy yourselves. It'll be good for her, too,' he added with a knowing smile.

'All right, then,' she said after a moment's hesitation.

It had occurred to her on more than one occasion during the week that if she allowed Melissa to get too close to Joel, it could break the little girl's heart when he left. On the other hand, they'd be able to console each other because Kirsten knew her own heart would definitely be breaking.

CHAPTER EIGHT

'How are you feeling today?' Kirsten asked Tony Watson, who had once again been left holding little Patrick while his wife went off to do something. Kirsten introduced Joel as they all entered the house and at least this time Patrick wasn't crying indignantly. It looked as though he'd just had a feed and was going off to sleep on his father's shoulder.

'Still tired,' he groaned as he continued to slowly rub his son's back. 'This has got to stop, Doc. You've got to make Gail come to her senses. She needs help. My mum has said she'd come around every day and help her out when I go back to work,' he added as they both sat down in the lounge room. 'Gail won't have a bar of her.'

'I think your mother may actually be part of the problem,' Kirsten said softly.

'What?'

'From what Gail said last week, your mother sees *Gail* as the problem, which isn't the case at all. Gail is a good mother and you are a good father but you need help from an outside source and the QE II family hospital is the best way to go. It's not only Gail who needs help, but *you* as well.'

Tony quickly shook his head. 'Nah. Not me, mate. I'm as right as rain. A bit tired, but I can cope.' He glanced at Joel. 'Us blokes can always cope. Isn't that right, mate?' he asked Joel.

'Not necessarily, and definitely not where babies are concerned. All those myths that say men have to be the stronger sex are irrelevant when it comes to fatherhood.

Why,' he added in a stage whisper, 'do you think it's the *women* who have the babies?'

Kirsten smiled at Joel's words and watched as Tony's face grew slightly pale.

'I have two brothers and one sister who have children, and all of them have found it equally as hard. It's doing it *together* that has made it easier for them.'

'Joel's made a good point,' Kirsten said. 'You and Gail need to pool your resources, to *rely* on one another, not play pass the baby.'

'Tell that to her,' Tony grumbled, his son now completely asleep on his shoulder.

'Has the past week been *any* better?' Kirsten asked.

'A bit but not much. Gail likes the house to be clean at all times and won't accept help from anyone. She thinks she's supermum or something like that and that she can cope, but she can't.' He sighed and rested his head back against the chair. 'I'm just sick of it,' he whispered, his eyes closed and tears peeping out from behind them. 'I'm tired of being responsible. I'm tired of trying to be in control. I'm tired of Patrick's crying and Gail's constant bad mood. I have to go back to work on Monday. I'll be falling asleep at my desk and then I'll probably get fired, which won't do *any* of us *any* good.'

Kirsten and Joel both waited. This was progress, and if they both kept quiet hopefully Tony would open up even more.

'My dad…' He sniffed and opened his eyes, looking past both of them and out into oblivion. 'My dad has always been the one to rule the family. He earned the money and my mum raised the kids. He would think I'm weak if he knew I was so out of control. You've got to take care of your family, son, he always says. That's the way it should be.'

'No.' Kirsten shook her head sadly. 'That's the way it

was. Nowadays, with mothers working just as much as fathers, it's definitely a combined effort. You *both* earn the money and you *both* raise the children. My brother and his wife have just had their first child and they're not finding it easy either, but there's one thing they always make sure they do and that's communicate. They touch base with each other every day. As soon as their son is asleep, they sit down and talk. If my brother is at work, my sister-in-law calls him on the phone. She puts notes in his lunch-box and his briefcase, reminding him of how much she loves him. They bath their son together, they've put him on one bottle of formula for the day so that Luke can give him a bottle, thereby being involved in the feeding process as well.'

'Sounds nice,' he said dryly. 'But, as you said, their son sleeps.'

'Intermittently,' Kirsten added. 'I understand that Gail wants the house kept tidy but at times like this it's better for her to conserve her energies. Hire a house-cleaner. It doesn't have to be for ever, just for a month.'

'I've already suggested that,' he said, and rested his head against the back of the chair again. 'I'm just sick and tired of trying. If Gail doesn't book herself and Patrick into that QE II hospital place, then I will. *I'll* take him and get him into a routine and Gail can just stay at home and sleep.'

'Now, *that's* something worth discussing,' Joel said enthusiastically.

'Let me go and find Gail,' Kirsten suggested. There was no way she was going to pass up this opportunity for the two of them to get their act together. Hopefully today they'd make more progress.

Within an hour, Gail and Tony had finally agreed to seek help. It hadn't been an easy process but having Joel there to swat away Tony's reservations had really helped. Gail had still been very reluctant but when Tony had declared he'd take another week or so off work and take Patrick to the hospital by himself, Gail had broken down in tears.

Perhaps this was what she'd been waiting for all along, a sign from her husband that they were in this together. Kirsten agreed to provide Tony with a medical certificate in case he needed to take the time off as sick leave. He called his office and was given the time off as extended paternity leave—his boss, having been through a similar situation not that long ago, was happy to accommodate the request.

'I wonder how many other men have been through this?' he said quietly to Joel.

'A lot more than either of us would suspect,' Joel answered with a nod.

June, the midwife, arrived ten minutes before Kirsten and Joel were due to leave for their next house call. As June knew more about the set-up at the hospital, Kirsten left all the little details with her.

'Next stop?' Joel asked.

'Canberra General to check on Ian Behr. It's been almost four weeks since he was electrocuted.'

'Wow! That long?' Joel said with a smile. 'Boy how time flies when you're having fun.'

'It certainly has been a busy four weeks,' Kirsten added, and briefly smiled at him as she navigated the traffic.

When they arrived at CGH, they made their way to the burns unit to see how Ian was doing. They both read his notes in the nurses' station before crossing to his bed. Stephanie had just left to run some errands but Ian was in high spirits.

'Well, if it isn't the people who saved my life,' he drawled with a smile. 'Good to see you.'

'You're certainly chirpy this afternoon,' Kirsten said, returning his smile, very happy to see that her neighbour was coping well with his situation.

'And why wouldn't I be?' he asked, obviously pleased about something special.

Kirsten tilted her head to the side. 'Are you going to tell us or keep us in suspense?'

'Well, my plastic surgeon, Mr Taylor, says I'm making an excellent recovery.'

'Excellent,' Joel said.

'That is good news but I'll bet it's not the news that's put that smile on your face.'

'Well, your brother Jed—' he looked at Joel '—said that my bones are well on track for almost a month after injury and that hopefully some time soon, depending on what Mr Taylor thinks, I should be able to go to the rehabilitation hospital before heading home.'

'Excellent prognosis,' Joel commented.

'No. That's not it,' Kirsten said as she peered more closely at Ian. She gasped softly and nodded her head. 'It's a girl. It has to be. I've lived next door to you for the past five years, Ian Behr, and I've grown to know that look in your eyes.'

Ian's grin grew wider in confirmation.

'Yep. Laura Hemmingway came to see me earlier today—she'd just finished an exam and had a free study session. She's in my English Literature class and I've been waiting for the perfect opportunity to ask her to the end-of-year dance. I didn't think I stood a chance.' He motioned to his body. 'Not with *these* injuries. I didn't think she'd want to know me at all.'

'I guess she feels quite the opposite,' Joel said.

'I guess you could say that,' Ian replied, the satisfied smirk on his face remaining in place. 'Although I can't go to the dance, she's agreed to come here or wherever I am and we can at least spend the evening together.'

'How romantic.' Kirsten sighed dramatically and Joel chuckled.

'Well, it's good to see you happy. Believe me, it will help your bones and your hands to heal faster.' Joel nodded.

'That's what your brother said.'

'It must be true, then,' Joel said. They stayed for a while longer before heading down to Orthopaedics to check on Frances Althorpe. Because of her fractured pelvis she was in traction and rather uncomfortable, but it didn't stop her from telling them the latest hospital gossip or passing on a few good jokes she'd heard.

'It's great to see patients recovering so well,' Kirsten said to Joel as they headed back to the car. 'Especially Frances. I kind of...well, feel responsible for her. You know, I helped rescue her.'

Joel hung his arm about her shoulders as they kept walking. 'It's an incredible feeling,' he agreed, and turned her face briefly so they could kiss. 'Mmm, you taste good,' he murmured as they reached her car. The weather, thankfully, had turned warmer and the breeze felt lovely across Kirsten's face.

She leaned back against the driver's door and looked up at Joel. He placed a hand on either side of her face and leaned in to kiss her more thoroughly. Once more the butterflies in Kirsten's stomach began to flutter around. Her knees began to weaken and she lifted her hands and slowly slid them up the firm contours of his chest before lacing her fingers behind his head.

'Mmm,' she groaned, and pulled back momentarily. 'You taste good, too.'

Joel grinned back at her and wiggled his eyebrows. 'I aim to please,' he whispered, capturing her lips again.

Kirsten breathed in suddenly at the strength of his kiss, the familiar scent of his aftershave teasing at her senses, drugging her inhibitions and making her feel as though this should last for ever. It had to. She loved him.

'Can't you two wait until you get home?' A deep male

voice, which sounded familiar, cut through their moment. They both turned to see Jed walking towards them. 'Honestly,' he chided mockingly as he waggled a finger at the pair of them, 'out here, in public. Tut-tut. I thought you both would have had better sense.'

Joel straightened up and gave his brother a hearty handshake. 'You're just jealous because Sally's not here.'

'Where is she?' Kirsten asked, a frown creasing her forehead as she carefully tested her knees, making sure they would support her, before moving away from the car.

'She flew to Sydney an hour ago. She's doing more wedding preparations with her mother.'

'Pining for her yet?' Joel quipped.

'Yes, as a matter of fact, I am,' Jed acknowledged readily.

'Ah, love,' Kirsten sighed.

'I'm heading home now, packing a bag and taking a taxi to the airport. We have a hectic weekend of wedding things to do.'

'Some guys have all the fun,' Joel commented, and Jed smiled good-naturedly.

'A man's gotta do what a man's gotta do,' he recited.

'Say hi to Mum and Dad for me,' Joel said as he shook hands with Jed again.

Kirsten leaned forward and kissed Jed on the cheek.

'Have fun,' she added. She climbed into the car and soon they were headed for the Dawsons' place—their last stop for the day. She was even beginning to look forward to dinner with Joel and Melissa.

'I'm really happy for Jed and Sally,' Kirsten said as she drove along.

'It's about time he settled down.' Joel agreed. 'After all, he is two years older than me—now, *that's* getting over the hill.'

'Hey, don't talk too soon. You'll be his age in two years' time.'

'Yeah, but he'll still be two years older.'

'Well, perhaps Jordanne looks at herself and thinks, Gee, I'm glad I'm not as old as Joel. I mean, there are six years between you two.'

'You and I as well, but the age difference doesn't seem to bother you.'

'Why would it?' she asked, her tone falling flat. You'll be gone soon, she added silently to herself.

'Alex is the same age as Jed,' he pointed out. 'That makes eight years difference between them, as well as eight years between Sally and Jed, so you and I aren't doing too badly.'

'Hmm.' She nodded, trying desperately not to attach any significance to his words. 'At least Jordanne and Alex have been able to work out their differences.'

'Is something wrong?' Joel asked, puzzled.

'Oh, I'm sorry. I thought you knew.' Kirsten clamped her mouth shut.

'You mean about conceiving a child?'

'Yes. It took them a while but they worked it out.'

'Just like Jordanne,' Joel said with a nod. 'Once she gets her teeth into something—'

'She doesn't let go,' Kirsten finished for him. 'And speaking of getting your teeth into something, Doris Dawson is going to be as pleased as Punch to see you again this week.'

'It's shameless how we flirt,' he added with a wide grin, and Kirsten laughed.

As she pulled into the Dawsons' driveway, she once more revelled in the beauty of the bottle-brush flowers. 'Look, they're starting to die off now.' She shook her head sadly as she looked down at the ground, but the green grass was covered with red stringy petals, turning it into another green and red festive sight. 'I love Christmas,' she said softly as Joel placed his hand on her shoulder.

'Only five and a half weeks to go,' he said. 'I'm especially looking forward to this Christmas. I haven't been able to get home for the past few years as I've always been training. At least this time the team is leaving *after* Christmas.'

The butterflies in Kirsten's stomach disappeared and in their place came twisted knots. 'Will you miss having a white Christmas?' she forced herself to ask, unable to look at him.

'No. Friends and family. This year, especially with Alex and Sally having joined our family, it will be more festive than normal. Mum said she's planning a big party.'

'I hope she doesn't overdo it—with the cooking and all, I mean.'

'She's a smart woman. She'll call in the caterers,' he said. 'What she does love doing is making her own name cards and bon-bons. I remember making them with her as a child. Jasmine and Justin couldn't stand the fiddling about but I loved it. She said it was the only way she could sit me down for hours and keep me entertained.' A deep chuckle rumbled forth and Kirsten felt the vibrations as his chest pressed into her back.

'Are you two coming into the house or do we have to come outside for our check-ups?' Doris called from the doorway.

'Sorry,' they both called, and headed for the door. Kirsten's nonchalant mood was instantly replaced with concern as she recognised the wheezing sound coming from inside.

Fred was sitting in his chair, a smile on his face, when they walked in the door. He raised one of Doris's biscuits to them in salute.

'You don't sound too good,' Kirsten said as she crossed

to his side. She opened her bag and took out her stethoscope.

'I'm fine, girl,' he replied with a cough. 'It's spring. Like you always say, it's the silly season for asthma sufferers.'

'Lift up your shirt,' she commanded.

'She's always been forward,' Fred joked as his gaze took in Joel. Kirsten didn't join in his merriment. Instead, she waited for him to comply. When he did, she listened to his breathing.

'Not good,' she told him when she was finished. 'Have you increased your preventative inhaler?'

'Yes, Doctor,' he rasped, the grin still on his face.

'I'm serious, Fred. This could turn nasty.'

'Bah, humbug,' he teased. 'I've had asthma all my life and I've learned how to deal with it. I'll be fine. I always get this way around this time of year.' He looked towards his wife. 'Don't I, Doris?'

'Yes, he does.' Doris nodded emphatically, although there was a look of concern on her face. 'Now, why don't you both sit down and have a biscuit? I've made them especially for you,' she crooned as she offered Joel the plate. He took one and after a bite he complimented her on her brilliant baking and mentioned that his mother wanted the recipe.

'Of course,' Doris replied. 'You know, Joel, you're so much like our son Simon,' she said. 'Isn't he, Fred?'

'Polite and charming,' Fred acknowledged as he helped himself to another biscuit.

'Go easy on those,' Kirsten warned.

'Now, listen here, Doc,' Fred said as he waggled the biscuit at her. 'I've always done everything you've suggested in the past and the future will be no different, but when it comes to my wife's biscuits I'll fight you tooth and nail if you tell me to give them up.'

Kirsten smiled at him and held up her hands in defence.

'All I said was to go easy.' She turned to face Doris. 'Now, I'd better get your check-up done before I get into any more trouble.' She laughed.

Doris rose to her feet, leaning heavily on the walking frame, while both Kirsten and Joel watched her closely.

'Very good,' Kirsten praised.

Next Doris displayed her walking techniques which once more had improved significantly since last week. 'How are the sessions with the physio coming along?' Kirsten asked.

Fred started coughing and they all turned to look at him. Some crumbs from his mouthful of biscuit were forced out as his body was racked with a spasm. He sucked in a breath, his eyes widening in terror as he tried once more to inhale. He gasped several times, each one a valiant attempt to breathe, but it was no good.

'He's choking on the biscuit,' Joel said as he rushed to stand behind Fred. He heaved the man out of his chair and struck him firmly between the shoulder blades, hoping to dislodge the obstruction. It was no good.

Kirsten was by his side and she quickly supported Fred while Joel performed the Heimlich manoeuvre. Nothing!

Fred kept trying to breathe in but only the smallest amount of air was getting through—and even that was becoming less.

'His glands are swelling. The biscuit won't budge.'

'Oh, dear,' Doris whispered, and Kirsten glanced over her shoulder at the other woman. Tears were streaming down her face. 'Oh, do something. Please? Please?'

'Get ready to lay him down, Kirsten,' Joel ordered as he reached for his medical bag. 'I'll do an emergency tracheostomy,' he said softly as he pulled on surgical gloves. Kirsten waited until he had everything ready before helping Fred to the ground.

'It's all right, Fred,' she told him. 'It's all right. We'll have you breathing normally in no time.' Kirsten watched Joel swab Fred's throat.

'What's he doing?' Doris asked in alarm as Joel picked up the scalpel.

'The biscuit is lodged too firmly. His throat is swelling up and he can't breathe. Joel is going to make a small cut into the trachea—that's the windpipe—so that air can get through to Fred's lungs. Otherwise he'll die of asphyxiation.'

'Oh, dear, oh, dear,' Doris wailed again.

Kirsten watched, praying silently as Joel made the incision, wiping the blood away with gauze. Once it was done, he inserted a piece of IV tubing that he'd cut off. It didn't work.

'The tubing's too small. I need something larger.' He looked at Kirsten, both of them thinking quickly.

'Ah… What…what about a funnel?'

'Do it.'

Kirsten stood and rushed to the kitchen. 'Help me out here, Doris,' she called. 'Where would I find a funnel?'

'Um…' Doris called from the living room as Kirsten began opening and closing cupboards left, right and centre. 'Um…cupboard next to the drawers down the bottom,' she finally managed.

'Got it,' Kirsten called, and rushed back. There was no time for sterilisation procedures as she quickly handed the funnel to Joel. He held it in place. A gurgling, rasping sound could be heard as Fred took a breath.

'Thank God,' Kirsten said softly, then smiled at the man she loved. 'Well done.' She unclipped her mobile phone from her waist and pressed the pre-set number for the ambulance. After she'd given them the particulars, she looked down at Fred. His eyes were closed tight in concentration as he listened to Joel's soothing words, which were helping him to breathe more easily.

'Is he all right?' Doris asked, and Kirsten stood, going to her side.

'He can breathe now.'

'Oh,' she sobbed. 'Thank you. Thank you.' She clutched her hands together and raised them heavenward.

'Come on, Doris. Let's go and pack a bag for Fred so that when the ambulance arrives he's already to go.'

'I'm going, too,' Doris told her firmly.

'Of course you are so we'll need a bag for you, too.'

When the ambulance finally arrived, they took over and were able to provide Fred with the proper tubing to allow him to breath through the tracheostomy. Kirsten and Joel followed the ambulance in her car and went through the rigmarole of getting Fred and Doris settled.

Fred was taken to Theatre where the ENT surgeon took over his care. The obstruction was removed and they both waited with Doris until Fred was out of Theatre and settled in ICU for the night. Knowing they were both in good hands, Kirsten and Joel wearily walked back to her car and headed for her home.

'Did you call your parents?' he asked as he looked at the dashboard clock. It was almost eight p.m.

'Yes. They took Melissa down to my house so she could have her dinner there. Here's hoping she eats more than last night.'

'Will she be ready for bed?'

'I don't think so. She hasn't been settling down to sleep until close to ten, even though we usually go to bed around eight-thirty.'

Joel reached over and placed his hand on Kirsten's knee. 'Things will settle down,' he prophesied.

'I hope so,' she sighed.

'Are you hungry?'

'Not really, but I think I should eat something.' It was

then that Kirsten remembered their earlier dinner plans. 'Joel?'

'Yes,' he replied with a knowing smile.

'Would you mind if we didn't go out for dinner? I'm exhausted.'

'I can see that. However, when we took Fred to hospital, I began thinking about plan B.'

Kirsten glanced at him briefly. 'I'm afraid to ask,' she murmured.

'It's a surprise.'

'Joel, promise you won't—'

'Trust me, Kirsten,' he said softly, and squeezed her knee. 'Just trust me.'

When they arrived home, Melissa was sitting on the lounge between Kirsten's parents, watching television.

'Hi, Lissy,' Kirsten said and bent down, holding her arms out wide. She wasn't disappointed and wondered whether she'd *ever* get used to the tightness of Melissa's squeeze when she hugged her.

When Melissa spied Joel standing behind Kirsten, she quickly let go and launched herself at him. Kirsten frowned as Joel picked the girl up and hugged her close. He really was becoming vastly important to her niece and she wasn't sure whether to stop it or encourage it. So far he'd managed to get smiles and giggles out of her more than anyone else. It was a definite step in the right direction but when he left…what would happen then? Would Melissa retreat once more? Would she understand that Joel had to go away and that they could watch him on the television? Would she understand that, although he hadn't died, he might not be coming back?

'Hello, mischief,' he said, and tickled her tummy. Melissa giggled a bit but still didn't say anything. 'Have you been a good girl today?'

Melissa nodded.

'Well, because you've been good today, I have a surprise for you.'

Melissa's eyes grew wide with excitement.

'We'd better get going,' Isobelle said as she and Greg stood. 'She didn't eat all that much.' Her tone was quiet. 'She might eat more with you and Joel. See how she goes.' They said goodnight to everyone and Kirsten hugged her mother close.

'Thank you,' she whispered in her ear. 'It's so good to know you're here to help.'

'We wouldn't have it any other way,' her mother said, and kissed her daughter's cheek.

When they were gone, Joel instructed Melissa to go and help Aunty Kirsten to change out of her work clothes into something a bit more comfortable. When she had dressed in a pair of comfortable shorts and T-shirt and Melissa had helped to brush her hair, the two of them returned to the lounge room. There they found the furniture pushed to the sides and a large red and navy picnic rug in the centre of the floor.

Cups and plates had been arranged but there was no sign of Joel.

'Joel?' Kirsten called tentatively, and when she heard a car door slam, she turned in the direction of her front door. It was open. 'What's going on?' she mumbled as she headed towards it.

'Joel?' she called again, and saw him walk down the driveway from a strange car that soon sped off into the night. She returned her attention to Joel who was carrying two bags. Kirsten felt a smile twitch at her lips. 'Plan B?' she asked as he came inside the house.

'Plan B.' He nodded. 'A picnic on the floor for three!'

Kirsten watched as he took Melissa through and started setting things up. It was perfect. Absolutely perfect. She didn't feel like going out and she hadn't felt like cooking.

He had also been right to suggest she relax a little bit more and this was the perfect way to do it.

Her heart overflowed with love, watching as he involved Melissa in the remaining jobs to be done, the four-year-old delighting in the responsibility.

'Come. Sit. Eat,' he commanded, and the three of them had a feast. Melissa ate some rice and a small piece of chicken, but dived into the prawn chips, eating almost every last one in the bag.

'I've never seen her eat this much,' Kirsten said in a conspiratorial whisper to Joel. 'I hope she doesn't overdo it.'

'We'll keep an eye on her,' he promised, and leaned over to kiss her. Kirsten loved the warm touch of his lips on hers. She smiled at him and they both turned to see Melissa watching them intently from very tired eyes.

Kirsten held out her arm and motioned to her. 'Come here, Lissy.'

Melissa did as she was asked and came and sat on Kirsten's knee. Joel's arms were now around both of them and Melissa snuggled close into Kirsten's soft curves before sighing with contentment.

'Family,' Melissa whispered, before closing her eyes and drifting off to sleep.

CHAPTER NINE

MELISSA'S one word—'family'—had caused a multitude of emotions to sweep through Kirsten. She was rejoicing that her niece was once more speaking and in the three weeks that had passed since Melissa had said that one word, the child hadn't stopped talking. The flood-gates had been opened.

On the other hand, the fact that she saw Joel as a substitute father raised alarm bells within Kirsten. She had no idea what to do. Melissa was so taken with Joel that to deny her access would be cruel.

Indeed, when Kirsten had gone to Canberra General Hospital for her emergency roster duty, Melissa had spent the day with Joel. Alex was pleased with Joel's knee recovery but still hadn't cleared him to return to the emergency roster, and as Kirsten's parents had driven to Sydney to visit her brother it had worked out well that Joel could look after Melissa.

When she'd returned home, late in the evening, she had walked through her house, calling to both of them. No answer. She'd crossed the back lawn to the cottage and through the open screen door she'd seen the two of them leaning back in Joel's reclining chair—both sound asleep.

Her heart had pounded wildly and her throat had constricted with emotion. *Her family*, she'd thought, and since then had worked hard to get that fantasy image out of her head.

Joel's knee had been improving dramatically and he was now walking well without the aid of his stick. He'd told her two days ago that the physio was extremely happy and had pronounced him right on target for his Christmas Eve try-out.

Kirsten had tried to be happy when he'd told her but knew it was one step closer to him leaving. He never talked about life *after* the Olympics and on a few occasions she'd actually tried asking him, only to chicken out at the last moment.

As she sat at her desk, her last patient gone for the morning, Kirsten thought once more of the right action to take. The problem was, the more time she spent with Joel, the more addicted she became. She'd told herself over and over again to just enjoy being with him but the niggling doubts still kept creeping back.

There was a knock on her door and Joel poked his head around. 'Ready?' he asked, dangling a set of car keys from his finger. When she nodded he said, 'Great, because I can't wait to try out my new car.'

'I don't understand why you bought one,' she reasoned, forcing her voice to sound calm. A calm she by no means felt. When she'd initially learned of his purchase, a ray of hope had sprung up within her that he might be willing to stay. That perhaps after the Olympics Joel would return to Canberra—to her and Melissa, so that they could become a family. She concentrated on downloading her files before switching off her computer.

'I didn't buy it, Kirsten,' he said, putting the keys in his pocket, and she looked up at him with a frown. 'I leased it. I thought I'd told you that.'

The hope that had built died a sudden death and she felt instantly bereft. 'No,' she said softly, and shook her head for emphasis.

'Sorry.' He frowned as she walked towards him. 'It must have slipped my mind in all the excitement.' He kissed her lips firmly and Kirsten was cross with herself for the way he made her feel faint. 'Come closer,' he murmured, and bent his head for another kiss—but not before he stepped into her office and shut the door behind him.

Kirsten sighed, willingly surrendering to him. She was powerless to resist, knowing his kisses and caresses were a drug and she was completely addicted. Heartache and heartbreak would come later and she'd just have to find some way of dealing with it. Right now she intended to take what she could.

His mouth moved over hers in a possessive fashion, his lips urgent and hungry. 'I feel as though we've hardly spent two seconds together during the past few weeks,' he murmured when he broke free to kiss the creamy expanse of her neck.

As it was now December and the weather outside nice and sunny, Kirsten was dressed in a white cotton sundress with inch-thick straps, revealing the satiny skin below her neck and above her cleavage.

When his kisses started to move lower, heading down towards the valley between her breasts, Kirsten groaned, her fingers lacing through his hair, her eyes closed in desire. Her breathing was ragged but when Joel's hands, which had been at her waist, moved a little higher and his thumbs began to caress the underside of her breasts, Kirsten gasped with pleasure.

Her knees started to give way and Joel must have felt it for he effortlessly picked her up and moved the short distance to her desk. He placed her gently on the tidy jarrah tabletop before bringing his mouth to hers once more.

Kirsten gave everything of herself to the kiss, her arms gathering his body as close as she could, her neck arching up to ensure their lips remained in contact. This was her way of showing Joel just how much she loved and cared for him.

During the past three weeks, they'd shared small touches and kisses when they could as both had hectic schedules.

Kirsten was busy concentrating on Melissa and work while Joel still had a lot of physiotherapy and training to undergo. Both of them had priorities elsewhere but Kirsten knew for sure that the chemistry that flared so vibrantly between them was something they needed to explore *if* they could find the time.

Joel's hands trailed sensually up and down her spine, causing Kirsten to shiver with delight.

'Mmm,' she sighed before he brought those masterful hands up to cup her face. He drew back slightly, his kisses now light and feathery—teasing her senses, leaving them begging for more.

'You're wonderful,' he growled as he nipped her lips once more. His eyes were glazed with a pent-up passion that she knew was mirrored in her own eyes. His breathing was ragged and uneven, as was her. His touch was tender as his thumb lightly caressed her swollen lips. 'Kirsten,' he breathed, their gazes locked. 'I've *really* missed you.' He pressed his mouth firmly to hers once more as though proving his words to be true. 'I can't get enough of you.' He bent his head and buried it in her neck. Breathing in deeply, he groaned, 'You smell divine. You feel unbelievable. You taste delicious.' He pretended to sink his teeth into her neck, his tongue flicking lightly against her skin.

Goose-bumps riddled her body at his touch and she decided it was pay-back time. Kirsten threaded her fingers through his dark hair, holding his head still before she slightly angled her head to nip with her teeth at his ear lobe.

He jerked his head up, smiling down at her in that devastating way that caused her stomach to churn and her pulse rate to accelerate. 'Do you have any idea how incredibly beautiful you are?'

'Do you have any idea how incredibly sexy you are?' she responded, her voice husky with affection.

'Oh, honey,' he murmured as his head began to descend again, 'you shouldn't say things like that.' His mouth was soft and sweet this time, moving slowly and sensually over her own.

'You shouldn't call me honey,' she whispered adoringly against his lips. 'It has a consuming effect on me.' She pressed her lips on his, her tongue tenderly slipping between them.

'Honey.' He kissed her. 'Sweet-heart.' Another kiss. 'Sugar-lips.'

'What?' Kirsten giggled as she pulled back to look at him. He was grinning at her as though he'd won the lottery.

'I like making you smile, *honey*.'

'You're very good at it, *sugar-lips*,' she returned.

Joel gathered her back into his arms, her head resting against his shoulder. 'I could stay here all day.'

'Mmm, I know what you mean… But that won't get the work done, nor will you be able to make it to the Olympics.' She felt his hold loosen at her words as he slowly released her.

'No, it won't.' He kissed her once more before lifting her to the floor. He raked a hand through his hair and frowned, turning his back on her to gaze out the window.

'You don't sound too enthusiastic,' Kirsten replied, instantly concerned about him. 'Is there something wrong?'

He was silent for a whole ten seconds which made Kirsten worry even more. 'Joel?' She crossed to his side and placed her hand on his arm, urging him around to face her. 'Joel? Is everything all right? Your knee?'

'My knee's fine,' he eventually said, a forced smile on his face. 'I'm fine.' He nodded and she wondered who he was trying to convince. Didn't he realise that she knew him better than that?

'I thought your training and physio were right on track,' she added.

'It is. There's just a lot going on, that's all. I'm fine,' he said again, and kissed her lips as though trying to prove it. 'Now, how about we get started on our house calls.' He pushed his hand into his pocket and pulled out his set of shiny new keys. 'Let's take my car.'

Kirsten tried to ignore her apprehension at his attitude, telling herself to think about it later. She forced a smile.

'Want to play with your new toy, eh?'

'If you want to call a Jaguar XJ8 a new toy, then you'd better believe I want to go and play with it.' He grinned. 'After all, I haven't driven a car since the beginning of August which is when I hurt my knee. Just let me get my medical bag and I'll meet you out front.' His eyes were alive with excitement again, as though the melancholy moment had never happened.

Their first stop was with the Watson family. Tony had returned to work after the entire family had spent a week at the Queen Elizabeth II family hospital.

'We're all so much better,' Gail said after she'd welcomed them in. Patrick was asleep in his pram while his mother looked brighter and happier than Kirsten had ever seen her. 'I don't know how to thank you—June as well—for your help. I know it's still not going to be easy but at least we're all sleeping better now.'

'Which makes the world of difference,' Kirsten agreed with a heartfelt nod. She'd slowly managed to get Melissa back into her own bed and even though the child was still wetting her bed, at least they were both getting more sleep than before.

'We've supplemented Patrick's feeds with two bottles of formula, one in the morning and one at night, as June said my milk was starting to dry up. This way, Tony gets to feed him and I get a break. It's wonderful.' Gail beamed at them, a happy and healthy mother.

'I'm so pleased for you,' Kirsten said. They talked some

more, and while they all drank tea Gail took every opportunity to talk about her wonderful son and husband while Kirsten and Joel simply smiled and nodded. When they'd finished their tea, Kirsten took Gail off to the bedroom for a check-up while Joel attended to Patrick who had woken up only moments before.

Gail was healing well after her episiotomy and there were no indications of mastitis or any other infections.

'What about the postnatal depression?' Gail asked a little hesitantly. 'Will it come back?'

Kirsten smiled. 'Your signs and symptoms have drastically decreased in the past few weeks and I would say that you'll be fine. On the other hand, if you feel that things are becoming a bit much, that you might not be coping as well as you'd thought, give either me or June a ring and we can organise for some extra help for you.'

'Tony's arranged for someone to come and clean the house once a week,' she admitted almost grudgingly. 'I'm very particular about my house and how it's cleaned.'

'I'm sure you are. I'm the same but even if it's just for the next few months, until Patrick is a bit older, it will hopefully alleviate some of your stress. Instead of fretting about the vacuuming, you can sit down and spend time simply playing with your son.'

'Sounds good.' Gail smiled at Kirsten as they headed out of the bedroom.

'It's really great to see them happy,' Kirsten said as she climbed into the passenger side of Joel's fancy new car. *Leased* car, she reminded herself.

'A job well done,' he told her with a nod. 'Where to next, Doc?'

'To the hospital, please. We'll check on Fred and Frances before heading out to the rehabilitation hospital to see Ian.'

'I wonder how his romance with…what was her name?'

'Laura Hemmingway,' Kirsten supplied, smiling.

'Ah, yes. Isn't young love grand?'

Kirsten didn't reply and forced herself to fix her smile in place when it wanted to disappear. She wished he wouldn't talk about things like love when she had no idea what was going to happen to *their* relationship.

'Here he is,' Doris said with an excited smile when Kirsten and Joel walked into Fred's private room. 'The man who saved my Fred's life,' Doris continued dramatically as she rose from her chair beside her husband's bed and held out her hand to Joel.

Kirsten chuckled and made room for Joel to pass. He walked over to Doris who tugged on his arm until he bent down low enough for her to kiss him on the cheek.

'Hey, watch it,' Fred whispered, his voice still raspy and hoarse. 'I might get jealous, you know.'

'Oh come off it, Freddie,' Doris said as she released Joel and clutched her husband's hand possessively. 'I only have eyes for you, my darling.'

Kirsten sighed romantically. 'True love,' she said wistfully, ensuring her gaze didn't meet Joel's. 'Well, I can see and hear that you're feeling better, Fred,' she remarked as she picked up his chart. 'Good.' She nodded. 'Very good. The ENT specialist is also pleased, even if it has taken you a bit longer to recover than the textbooks say.'

'Then again,' Joel added, 'what would a textbook know?'

'Exactly,' Kirsten said with a satisfied nod as she handed Fred's chart over to Joel.

'How much longer is he going to be in?' Doris asked as she sat back down in her chair.

'Can't wait to have him home again?' Joel asked with a laugh.

'Ooh yes,' Doris said in an exaggerated tone. 'I miss having to pick up his smelly socks and refilling my biscuit tins all the time.' Although she said it jokingly, they all knew there was a lot of truth in her words. 'Oh, here,' she said as she took a piece of paper out of her bag and handed it to Joel. 'Here's the recipe for your mother. All I ask in return is for one of hers.'

'It's a deal,' Joel said with a smile, before turning back to Fred. 'And you…make sure you take it easy on the biscuits from now on,' he warned good-naturedly.

'I will, Doc,' Fred replied solemnly.

'Whenever his asthma is bad, I'm going to soak the biscuits in milk so they're nowhere near as hard and crunchy,' his wife announced with a firm nod of her head.

'That's what she's been threatening to do,' he said with a resigned shrug.

'If it works…' Kirsten left the sentence hanging as she walked around the bed to take a closer look at Fred's throat. 'Healing nicely.'

'The big chief doctor was most impressed with Joel's cut,' Doris told them. 'He said you did a mighty fine job.' Doris looked sweetly at Joel.

'Thank you. I did receive a letter from him about Fred's surgery and his progress, which was nice,' he said matter-of-factly as he took his turn to look at Fred's wound site.

As he was closer, Kirsten handed him a stethoscope and Joel listened to Fred's chest. 'Asthma's settled down, too.'

'He'll live,' Kirsten told Doris.

'Oh, I know that. Fred wouldn't dare die without asking me first,' she told them, 'but when can I take him home?' There was a pleading tone in her voice now.

'I'll go and check with the ward sister,' Kirsten said, and headed off to the nurses' station. When she returned, it was with some visitors in tow—two of Fred's and Doris's children, along with the grandchildren, had come to visit them.

'Look who I found,' she said as she held the door into the room, allowing Fred's family to precede her. They all greeted each other with hugs and kisses—another close family, she mused.

'What did Sister say?' Doris asked, shushing everyone for a moment.

'If everything looks as good as it does today, he should be able to go home after the surgeon has done his morning rounds.'

'Ooh, that's wonderful news.' Doris' face was alive with happiness as she beamed down at her husband. 'Thank you, Kirsten, dear, and you too, Joel. We are for ever in your debt. If there's ever anything we can do, let us know.'

'Well…' Kirsten said thoughtfully, 'you can allow me to come and admire your garden when I make my house calls.'

'And how about some freshly baked biscuits?' Joel said as he rubbed his stomach.

'You've got a deal,' Fred and Doris said together.

'We'll be around to check on you on Thursday next week,' Kirsten told them both. 'But you call me if you need me sooner,' she added.

'Is there a problem?' Doris asked.

'A big one,' Joel teased, rolling his eyes. 'My big brother is getting married next weekend and both Kirsten and I are in the bridal party.'

'We're all flying to Sydney next Friday for the rehearsal and pre-wedding events,' Kirsten added.

'Ooh, how exciting. Is this your brother who also works here in the hospital? The one who's good friends with Dr Page?'

'Yes. Both Jordanne and Alex are in the wedding party too. It'll be interesting to see how Canberra General copes without four of its best orthopaedic surgeons,' Kirsten joked.

'All right, then, dears. We'll see you next Thursday.'

Kirsten and Joel said goodbye, leaving them to celebrate

the good news of Fred's release with their family, and made their way to the orthopaedic department. When they arrived, Kirsten went to the bed which Frances Althorpe had occupied and was amazed to see it empty.

'She's been transferred to the rehab hospital,' the ward sister told her when she enquired.

'That's good news. She must have been doing well.'

'Yes, she was,' Alex said from behind them, and Kirsten and Joel turned to face him.

'Hi,' she said, and smiled. Alex and Joel shook hands.

'Checking up on Frances?' Alex asked.

Kirsten nodded. 'And Fred Dawson.'

'I saw Fred and Doris earlier today,' Alex said.

'Why?' Joel asked, then snapped his fingers. 'That's right,' he continued, answering his own question. 'You're Doris's orthopaedic surgeon as well as Jordanne.'

'Yes. Doris's hip is healing perfectly and Fred's doing quite nicely as well. Although I was a bit worried about how Doris would cope at home by herself, with Fred being in hospital for so long, but then I remembered they'd had six children. What's the point in having that many kids if they don't come around to help out in situations such as these?'

'Why do you think *my* parents had that many?' Joel laughed.

'It *is* nice to see their family supporting them,' she added. 'So Frances was well enough to be transferred?'

'Absolutely,' Alex replied. 'That woman has made the fastest recovery from multiple trauma that I've ever seen. She'll still need a lot of work but, considering her injuries, she'll be making it in record time.'

'She's always had a positive attitude,' Kirsten said. 'Even when she was buried, she made light of the situation.'

'It always helps. The brain is a powerful organ and if

you keep telling yourself that you're going to get better, nine times out of ten you do!' Alex's pager beeped and he glanced down at the number. 'I'm due in a meeting,' he said with resignation. 'If I don't see either of you before, see you in Sydney.' Alex hurried out of the ward and Joel and Kirsten weren't far behind him.

Once they were back in Joel's new car, driving in air-conditioned comfort, Kirsten leaned her head back against the head-rest and closed her eyes.

'Tired?' he asked after a moment.

'Mmm,' she murmured. 'I'm starting to get a headache. Nothing that an early night wouldn't fix.'

'Let's make sure you have one,' he said as he turned into the rehabilitation hospital car park. They saw Frances, who was happy to be in a new location. Her mood was bright and jovial as she showed off her range of motion.

'By Christmas-time, I'll be as good as new,' she told them. 'That's going to be my present to myself. A night at home with all my family and friends where I can boogie the night away.'

'Ah, don't go *that* far,' Joel cautioned. 'Perhaps a little waltz or a soft-shoe shuffle but no spinning on the floor unless you've had clearance from Alex.'

'Yes, Doctor,' she said, with the biggest grin on her face, showing she wasn't going to take any notice of him. 'I promise to speak to Alex about it.'

'I guess that's all I can ask,' he said with a resigned shake of his head.

Ian was in just as good spirits as Frances, although perhaps it had something to do with Laura Hemmingway sitting by his bedside.

'We can't stay too long,' Kirsten told her neighbour, who was looking extremely well.

'What a pity,' he said without sincerity.

Kirsten and Joel both read his chart and took a look at his hands.

'They look fantastic,' Kirsten said, satisfied with the situation.

'Yeah, they do. Well, it was nice of you to drop by,' Ian said, and they took their cue, leaving him alone with Laura.

Joel drove them back to Kirsten's house and then walked with her up the street to collect Melissa. While they were walking, his mobile phone rang and Kirsten tensed, hoping it wasn't the hospital or anything to do with their patients.

Whoever it was, the call was brief and he ended it just as Isobelle opened the door, leaving Kirsten no time to ask who it had been.

'You're home early,' Melissa squealed as she launched herself first at Joel and then at Kirsten. Whenever he was around, he always came first. Which, she guessed, shouldn't have surprised her as Melissa had enjoyed a wonderful relationship with her own father. She remembered Jacqui saying that Melissa had definitely been Daddy's girl. Now, it seemed, she was Joel's girl.

Kirsten pushed the niggling doubts to the back of her mind and forced a smile for the child. True to his word, Joel had them both fed and in bed by half past eight. He tucked Melissa in, read her a story, said prayers with her and gave her a goodnight kiss, before switching on her night-light and leaving her to sleep.

Then he walked into Kirsten's room and tucked her into bed—*very* thoroughly—before stroking his fingers through her loose hair, looking down into her eyes.

'Kirsten, that phone call I received earlier…'

She held her breath, prickles of apprehension winding their way throughout her body. 'Yes?'

'It was the head coach of the team.'

She couldn't speak. Her vocal cords were paralysed, her eyes as wide as saucers. He must have read the concern on her face because he quickly bent his head to claim her lips. 'Relax. It's nothing bad. I just have to go to Sydney for some final tests. There's an indoor snow arena where we can do the tests necessary to see how my knee performs before the coach can make up his mind.'

'But I thought you had until Christmas Eve?' she whispered brokenly.

'I do, but this will at least give the coach an idea of how things have progressed.'

Kirsten fought back the tears, feeling such a fraud. Joel had thought she'd been concerned about his knee and his ability to perform well, but she hadn't. She'd been more concerned for herself and Melissa.

'When do you go?' she asked.

'Tomorrow. I'll need the week in Sydney and then we can see each other again on Friday for the wedding rehearsal.' He smiled down at her.

'So you're leaving us,' she whispered accusingly, unable to stop the tear that squeezed itself out and rolled down her cheek.

'Hey, hey,' he soothed, and brushed it tenderly away. 'I'll only be gone for six days and then we've got a hectic weekend with the wedding.' He bent to kiss her lips but she didn't respond.

He was going—just as she'd known he would. It might only be for six days this time but it would be longer the next time. Who knew? It might be for good.

CHAPTER TEN

'YOU look *awful*,' Sally said when she dropped around to see Kirsten on Sunday evening. Kirsten sneezed as she closed the door behind her friend.

'It's a virus,' she told Sally. 'Great word, that. Virus.' Kirsten sneezed again and blew her nose. 'Don't get too close. You don't want to be sick for the wedding.'

'That's a whole six days away,' Sally said as she waltzed into the kitchen and plugged the kettle in. 'Sit down and put your feet up,' her friend ordered in her best 'doctor's' voice. 'Where's Melissa?'

'Having a little nap.'

'She has this, too?'

Kirsten nodded. 'Where do you think *I* got it from? I've been taking her to a playgroup for the past few Thursdays and—' She sneezed again. 'After last Thursday, she came down with a high temperature yesterday afternoon.'

'Just after Joel left?' Sally asked softly as she wandered around Kirsten's kitchen, getting out crockery to make a cup of tea.

A lump formed in Kirsten's throat and she realised she couldn't speak. He'd been gone for twenty-four hours and now both of them were sick. Didn't that say something? She nodded then rested her head back against the lounge and closed her eyes. She felt awful. Hot, tired and one hundred per cent cross with Joel for leaving them. Couldn't he see that they both loved him? That they both needed him?

'She got the temperature first and then last night she couldn't keep any food down. At first, I thought she was pining for Joel,' she said after a while, trying to hold back the tears. Sally brought the tea over and placed it on the coffee-table. 'Now I think it's a virus.'

'So Melissa misses him?' Sally asked softly.

Kirsten opened her eyes and looked at her friend. 'After he'd driven off, Melissa turned to me and asked if he was going to come back.' Her bottom lip wobbled.

'What did you say?'

'I wasn't sure what to say.' Kirsten dabbed at her eyes with a clean tissue before blowing her nose. 'So I told her that we'd be going on an aeroplane to see him at the end of the week.'

Sally nodded. 'How did she take that?'

'Not too well. She ran to her bedroom and cried. This morning, she asked me if Joel had gone to heaven like her mummy and daddy...' Kirsten broke off on a choked sob. 'I don't think I can do this,' she cried, and Sally gathered her close.

'Can't do what?'

Kirsten pushed Sally away. 'No, don't. I don't want you getting sick.'

'Oh, shush,' Sally ordered with a smile. 'I'll be fine. I already had this virus two weeks ago.'

'You can get it again,' Kirsten said. 'Then you'll be sick for your wedding and that will be another responsibility I'll have to contend with.'

'No, you won't. Besides, it's only a twenty-four-hour virus and if I *were* to get it again, it would be well and truly over by Saturday.'

'You're a good friend.' Kirsten sobbed into Sally's shoulder before lifting her head and wiping her eyes. Her nose was raw from blowing it all the time and her eyes were itchy.

'You look as though you could use some sleep. Have you called your parents?'

'Yes. They know Melissa was a little off colour but we all thought that was because Joel had left.'

'He'll be back,' Sally said firmly. 'Right now, though, you're going to bed.'

'But Melissa will be waking any minute now.'

'Drink your tea,' Sally instructed, and handed Kirsten the cup. 'When did you last take paracetamol?'

'An hour ago.' Kirsten sipped at the liquid and realised it wasn't an ordinary cup of tea. It had honey and lemon and something else. She couldn't quite put her finger on the elusive ingredient.

'A drop of Tabasco sauce,' Sally supplied when Kirsten frowned and looked into the cup. 'Jane McElroy recommended it when I was sick and it works like a charm.'

Kirsten took another sip and screwed up her nose.

'Drink it,' Sally growled.

When Kirsten had finished, Sally helped her up and got her settled in her bed. 'Now, go to sleep. I'll stay and take care of everything.'

'I'm glad you came over,' Kirsten said softly as she thankfully closed her eyes, snuggling into the pillow. 'Why did you?' she asked a moment later, a frown on her face.

Sally laughed. 'Well, first of all, I *like* spending time with you. Secondly, I haven't seen too much of you lately, thanks to my wedding plans, and, thirdly, I wanted to ask Melissa to be my flower-girl.'

Kirsten smiled at her friend and closed her eyes again. 'That's nice, Sally. *Really* nice.' With that, she drifted off into a dream world, where Joel was by her side, gazing adoringly down at her. They were in a garden, surrounded by beautiful flowers, and she was dressed in a flowing white gown. It wasn't *Sally* who was getting married—it was *her*. There was Joel, in his black tuxedo, looking incredibly sexy, promising to love and cherish her for the rest of her days. Kirsten sighed and wondered whether dreams really *did* come true.

The following Friday, Kirsten was never more glad to get off a plane in her life. Both she and Melissa had endured an awful week without Joel but she also knew it was a taste of what was to come when he went away.

She had also come to terms with the fact that she was now a single parent—and she didn't like it one bit. Her parents were a great support but she'd felt the weight of her responsibility for Melissa even more this week, without Joel around.

Every night, Melissa had asked if Joel had gone to heaven. Whether he was coming back. They'd both cried and cuddled each other to sleep. The little girl had even had a recurrence of her nightmares which had previously started to decline.

Kirsten carried her handbag and camera case on one shoulder, while balancing a sleeping Melissa on the other, as she made her way off the plane at Sydney airport. With Melissa's behaviour bordering on hysteria that morning when they'd started out for the airport, Kirsten had had no option but to ask her father, who'd been driving, to stop at a pharmacy so she could buy some medicine that would help Melissa to relax.

Isobelle had even offered to change their flights, which were booked for the next morning, but Kirsten had declined. Jordanne would meet her at the airport and take her to Sally's parents' house. It was a large mansion which had plenty of rooms for guests. All the bridal party were staying over for the weekend.

'Here, let me take her,' a deep voice said, and Kirsten's heart pounded wildly against her ribs.

'Joel?' she whispered, and felt the blood drain from her head. She stumbled but he placed a protective arm around her before leading her to a chair. When she'd sat down, he gently took Melissa from her, cradling the sleeping child lovingly.

'Wh-what...?'

'What am I doing here?'

Kirsten nodded, her jaw still hanging open at the surprise of seeing him there. 'Jordanne was going to pick us up.'

'I told her I'd come.' He frowned. 'I thought I'd told you that I'd pick you up.'

Kirsten dropped her gaze to the carpet, glad her breathing was slowly returning to normal—well, as normal as it could be around Joel. She didn't want him to know that she'd specifically asked Jordanne to collect them so that she'd have a few more hours to get herself together before seeing Joel.

Her feelings towards him had been very mixed up—anger, frustration, annoyance and a desperate longing to have his arms about her again, to feel his lips pressed firmly to hers, to hear him murmur words of love that would bind and commit them to each other for an eternity.

Yet now that he was here, sitting beside her, all the negative emotions vanished and the only thing she could rationally concentrate on was how passionately she loved him. She looked up into his eyes and took a deep breath, a cleansing breath that made her smile.

'I've missed you,' she whispered, and leaned over to brush her lips seductively across his. Her eyes fluttered closed at the contact and she sighed.

'I've missed you, too,' he said when she pulled back. He bent his head and kissed Melissa's forehead. 'I've missed her as well.'

He looked into Kirsten's eyes. He looked as though he'd hardly slept for a few days and she belatedly remembered the rigorous training he'd probably been doing since his arrival last weekend. She cleared her throat. 'How's the knee?'

'Perfect,' he told her, but his smile didn't reach his eyes. Melissa started to stir and they both turned their attention to her. She rubbed her eyes and slowly opened them, only to look directly into Joel's.

'Hi, sweetheart,' he crooned, and sat her up.

Melissa threw her arms about his neck and buried her face there. 'You're here?' she said, and kissed him. She looked over at Kirsten. 'You were right, Aunty Kirsten. Joel *didn't* go to heaven like Mummy and Daddy.' She snuggled into him as though she'd never let him go again. Kirsten couldn't blame her. It was exactly the way she felt.

Kirsten saw Joel's sharp turn of his head and their gazes met. 'What?' he mouthed, his eyes filled with concern.

She shook her head. 'Don't worry about it. I think it's time we found our suitcases, isn't it, Lissy? Can you remember what colour yours is?' But when Kirsten looked at the little girl, her eyes were closed again, her head resting on Joel's shoulder, her arms wound tightly around his neck.

'Is she asleep again?' he asked, and Kirsten nodded. 'Hasn't she been sleeping too well?'

Kirsten shrugged. 'We've been all right. I had to give her some promethazine—just a small dose—for the flight.'

'Why?'

'She was hysterical about getting on the plane.'

'Why?' he asked again.

'She wouldn't say anything but I think it was because we were coming back to Sydney. It *was* her home for four years.'

He nodded and rose from the chair. 'Let's go and see about your luggage.'

Melissa woke up again and once more was glad to see Joel, smothering him with tiny kisses. He laughed heartily and draped an arm about Kirsten's shoulders. 'I'm so glad you're here.'

Melissa 'helped' him to push the trolley with their luggage on all the way to where the car was parked. It was a white Jaguar XJ6 which she recognised as belonging to Jed. Kirsten was glad of the four-year-old's company as she chattered on about all sorts of things and how she and Aunty Kirsten had been sick.

'Really?' Joel asked quietly, glancing over at Kirsten in the front passenger seat.

She nodded but didn't say anything else. At least Sally had been right—it had been a twenty-four-hour virus.

Joel reached over and placed his hand on her knee. 'It sounds as though you've had a bad week.'

'Mmm,' she said, holding her tongue. It wasn't really his fault that she'd come to rely on him so much, that she'd missed him so much, that she *loved* him so much.

'And Sally came over and looked after Aunty Kirsten and she asked *me* to be a flower-girl,' Melissa continued. 'And we had to have special icy-poles, didn't we, Aunty Kirsten? And mine was red and Aunty Kirsten's was orange and I had a red tongue and she had an orange tongue. Didn't you, Aunty Kirsten?'

'That's right,' Kirsten acknowledged with forced joviality. 'Tongue colour is *very* important when you're four years old,' she said in a conspiratorial whisper to Joel.

Melissa commanded his attention once more and told him about a friend she'd met at playgroup. When they arrived at the Bransford mansion, Sally rushed out to greet them. Melissa ran to her, allowing herself to be enveloped in a big hug.

'Whew!' Joel said as he climbed from the car and rubbed his ear. Kirsten laughed and nodded.

'I know what you mean. First we couldn't get her to talk and now we can't get her to stop, but I wouldn't want it any other way,' she said lovingly as she looked at her niece. They went inside and were shown to their rooms, Melissa oohing and aahing as they walked through the mansion.

The rest of the day had been planned to perfection and everyone enjoyed it. The grounds had been meticulously attended to and there was a beautiful marquee where the reception for five hundred people would take place. Caterers seemed to be everywhere, setting things up, polishing and preening.

'Only five hundred people?' Kirsten teased Sally that night when the three girls sat down in the garden to enjoy the sunset. Joel was busy putting Melissa to bed and Kirsten loved the feeling of relying on him again, even though she told herself not to. Surely this once would be all right?

'I was as surprised as you,' Jordanne said. 'After all, this is the great Norman Bransford's daughter getting married. I'd have thought he'd want to shout it from the rooftops.'

Sally laughed. 'The *old* Norman Bransford would have but he respects our wishes that we want it kept simple.'

Kirsten and Jordanne looked at each other with raised eyebrows. 'Five hundred is simple?'

'Hey, it was a compromise,' Sally said defensively.

'The rehearsal went well,' Jordanne said.

'You're going to have a perfect day,' Kirsten chimed in.

The three of them looked at each other and smiled. 'We've all been through so much,' Sally said, tears starting to gather in her eyes. 'Tomorrow is going to be so special for me and I'm so glad you're both going to be a part of it.'

They all held hands and squeezed. This was what friendship was all about, Kirsten thought.

Jordanne let go and jumped to her feet. 'Enough mushy stuff,' she said as she swiped at her eyes, 'because the last thing we want is to cry our eyes out, reminiscing about the past, causing all three of us have red and puffy faces tomorrow.'

'Good point,' Sally said. 'Any news on those fertility tests?' she asked Jordanne frankly. Kirsten knew that Jordanne expected nothing less. Their friendship was honest and open.

Jordanne shrugged. 'Alex says the results are better than the tests he had done before so that's a positive sign.'

'I should hope so,' Sally replied. 'He had those tests done almost twenty years ago during his first marriage. You two should be fine to have a family. With all the advances in medical technology in the last few years, how could you not be?' she finished.

'I agree. You and Alex will make wonderful parents,' Kirsten added, feeling a sudden sense of maternal pride at her *own* little girl who was hopefully falling asleep right now.

'How about you and Joel?' Jordanne asked.

Kirsten groaned and buried her face in her hands before peeking through her fingers at her friends. 'Don't ask or *I'll* be the one with red and puffy eyes tomorrow.'

'That bad? What's the problem? He loves you. My big brother loves you, I'm certain of it,' Jordanne proclaimed.

'I'm glad *somebody* is, because *he* doesn't seem to be.'

'You should have seen him when he found out Jordanne was going to get you and Melissa from the airport,' Sally said.

'He flipped his lid,' Jordanne said with a nod. 'He raved on about how he'd mentioned that he'd pick you up and that it was therefore his responsibility.'

'He demanded that Jed hand over his car keys and stormed out before anyone could say another word.'

'That still doesn't do me any good. For all we know, he was anxious to see Melissa.'

Jordanne and Sally both shook their heads. 'Nope. He's fallen big time for you,' Jordanne said.

'Well, I wish *someone* would tell him that!' Kirsten retorted.

The wedding was a spectacular affair, as they'd all expected it to be. Sally was the most beautiful bride in a simple but elegant off-white gown made of raw silk. It was a straight dress which emphasised her perfect figure. On top of her short blonde hair, Sally wore a diamond tiara with a veil. This headdress was the same one Sally's mother had worn on her wedding day. In her arms she carried a large bunch of bright yellow roses, yellow being her favourite colour.

Kirsten and Jordanne were dressed in yellow raw silk, each carrying a bunch of white roses. As both had long hair, Sally had requested they simply clip it back with a diamond-studded clip. Again, simple and elegant, which was the bride to a T. Melissa wore a pale lemon dress and carried a bunch of multicoloured baby roses, her blonde hair curled into ringlets.

The chairs had been set out in the garden, coloured roses in baskets lining the aisle. Jed stood waiting impatiently with Alex and Joel beside him. All three men looked devastatingly handsome in black tuxedos with bright yellow waistcoats. The weather was perfect for an outdoor wedding and thankfully not very humid for mid-December.

Everything seemed to happen in a blur, but when Jed and Sally faced each other, their hands entwined to say their vows, Kirsten couldn't help but glance in Joel's direction. She gasped softly when she realised he was looking at her, his gaze showing an emotion she'd never seen before. She tried hard to decipher it but all too soon she was following the happy couple back down the aisle, her hand firmly nestled in the crook of Joel's elbow.

'Lovely ceremony,' he said in her ear afterwards as everyone mingled.

'Definitely,' Kirsten had time to answer before Melissa tugged at her dress.

'I can't remember where the toilet is,' she said urgently, and Kirsten smiled at Joel and took her niece's hand.

When they returned, it was time for the wedding feast. Everyone sat down to devour the delicious food, leaving little time for Joel and Kirsten to talk. After the speeches, in which Jed spoke lovingly about his wife, the band started to play.

Melissa was beginning to tire and climbed up on Kirsten's knee. 'You've had a busy day, haven't you, darling?'

She nodded. 'It's been a lot of fun. My mummy would have liked it.' The words were said with a sad resignation and a lump formed in Kirsten's throat. It was good that they could talk about Jacqui and her husband. Indeed, it was something Kirsten was determined to continue—to keep the memories alive.

'Yes, she would have, darling.'

'Do you miss my mummy?' Melissa asked, and glanced up at her aunt.

'Very much,' Kirsten whispered, 'but you are so much like her that every time you smile I feel as though she's here with me.' She placed a hand over her heart. 'Always.'

'I love you, Aunty Kirsten,' Melissa said with a yawn.

'I love you, too, Lissy,' she whispered brokenly, fighting the tears that threatened to spill over and smudge her make-up.

Joel came over and sat in the seat next to Kirsten, looking down at the child now sleeping in her arms. 'It's been a big day for her. She's done well to make it this far.'

Kirsten smiled. 'Yes, she has.'

'Why don't I carry her to bed then you and I can come and dance?'

'What if she wakes up? She won't know where she is.'

Isobelle chose that moment to come over and kiss her granddaughter's head. 'She's beaten me to it.' She laughed. 'Your father and I are heading back to our lovely room now. I just wanted to say goodnight.'

Kirsten's mother looked from her to Joel and back again. 'Why don't I get Greg to carry Melissa back and we can keep an eye on her while she sleeps? She's only across the hall and that way you two can stay and enjoy yourselves.'

'Brilliant idea, Isobelle,' Joel said as he stood. 'I'll get Greg now.'

The whole thing was organised before Kirsten could protest. Although she loved Joel with all her heart, she felt a little uncomfortable being around him just now. There were too many uncertainties in their relationship and tonight definitely wasn't the place to discuss them.

'Come on, honey,' he said once her parents had carried Melissa away. He took her hand in his and led her to the dance area. 'Let's dance!'

On Sunday, Kirsten, Joel and Melissa all returned to Canberra. Jed and Sally were planning to spend several days in the beautiful Blue Mountains just west of Sydney before returning on the twenty-fourth of December for Jane McElroy's traditional tree-trimming party. This year Jane was planning to make it a large celebration.

'When will you be closing down the surgery?' Joel asked on Wednesday morning as he prepared to go to the institute for his last physio session.

'On Friday afternoon—until then it's business as usual,' she assured him as she finished eating her breakfast. Since their return she'd done everything possible to put her niggling doubts about their relationship to the back of her mind, but they kept forcing themselves back to the front again. She was trying to enjoy every minute she and Melissa could have with Joel, knowing he might soon be gone for ever.

She cleared her throat. 'When…uh…are you planning on going back to Sydney?'

'Friday evening. What flights are you and Melissa booked on?'

'We're not leaving until early Saturday morning. My parents will be flying with us this time, so hopefully I won't need to sedate her.'

Joel hesitated for a brief moment before asking, 'Did she *really* think I wasn't coming back?'

Kirsten looked directly into his blue eyes. 'Yes, Joel. She did,' she stated matter-of-factly. She knew how important this Olympic medal was to him, and because she loved him she only wanted his happiness, but couldn't he see that true happiness was right in front of him? She and Melissa loved him so much yet still he was searching for happiness elsewhere. When he didn't say anything else, Kirsten took her cup and plate to the sink.

'I'll do the dishes later. Right now I'd better get Melissa over to my mother's before I'm late for work.'

On Thursday, they spent the evening together, cuddling on the lounge and watching an old Mae West video after Melissa had gone to bed. Kirsten knew she'd treasure these times and memories with Joel for ever. He'd come into her life almost nine weeks ago and they'd been the best nine weeks of her life.

On Friday evening they took him to the airport as Kirsten had decided it was better for Melissa to see him get onto a plane than for him to drive away from their house in a taxi. She kissed him fondly before they watched the aeroplane take off into the sky.

'We'll see Joel tomorrow, won't we, Aunty Kirsten?' Melissa asked cautiously when they returned to the car.

'Of course we will, darling.'

As they drove along, Melissa was unusually silent and Kirsten began to worry that she might get sick again. Finally the little girl said, 'Why doesn't Joel live with you and me? You know, like Mummy and Daddy lived together.'

Kirsten tried to swallow, her throat suddenly dry. 'Well, darling, Joel and I aren't married.'

'But you kiss all the time.'

She smiled. 'Yes, yes, we do.'

'And you *like* him.'

'Yes.'

'And he likes you.'

'Yes.'

'But you haven't had a big wedding like Sally and Jed did, have you?'

'No, we haven't,' Kirsten responded, wondering whether they ever would have one or whether Olympic gold would be enough to keep Joel warm on those cold wintry evenings he was so fond of.

'Maybe you will one day and I can be in it, just like I was in Sally and Jed's wedding,' Melissa chattered on. 'And I think I'd like to wear a pink dress this time. Is Jordanne getting married soon?'

'Yes.' Kirsten tried not to let the pain show through in her answer. Both of her friends were happy with their soul mates, while *her* soul mate had just flown away—again!

'Maybe I'll be in Jordanne's wedding. I could wear a red dress in her wedding. Who is she marrying again? I forget.'

'Alex.'

'That's right. Alex. I can wear a red dress then and a pink dress when you get married, and I already have a yellow dress.' She thought about it for a moment before asking, 'Who else is getting married? I need a blue dress, too.'

Kirsten couldn't help but chuckle, the child breaking the sombre mood that had been settling around her. 'Darling, you don't need to be in a wedding to have a new dress. If you want a blue one, I'll buy one for you.'

'Wow, that would be fun, Aunty Kirsten, but a wedding is a lot more of a fun way to get a new dress.'

Kirsten sighed again. 'Yes, I suppose it is.'

Melissa continued to chatter on and was very easy to coax into bed that evening, with the promise of flying on a plane to see her beloved Joel the next day. This time there were no hysterics and, with her grandparents there, Melissa survived the short flight from Canberra to Sydney without getting bored—but only just!

This time Joel wasn't at the airport to greet them and Kirsten felt her heart plummet. Melissa's constant questioning as to his whereabouts didn't help. Instead, John McElroy had come to collect them, saying that Joel was currently undergoing his final test for the Olympics.

'I thought that wasn't until this afternoon?' Kirsten queried.

'He managed to get it changed. That way it's done and we can all enjoy the rest of the day.'

Melissa proceeded to be cautious around John, but once she got over her initial shyness she plied him constantly with questions.

When they arrived at the McElroys' home, Kirsten and Melissa were shown to Jordanne's old room.

'Oh!' Melissa gasped when she saw the beautiful room with a frilly bedspread and floral wallpaper. 'This is so lovely.'

Kirsten watched as the child stood in the middle of the room and just looked, her mouth wide open in wonderment. 'Would you like to decorate your room at home so it looks something like this?' she asked a little hesitantly. She'd specifically kept it the way Jacqui had set up Melissa's room because she thought it might help Melissa adjust.

'Can we?' she asked hopefully.

'Of course, darling. After Christmas, we'll go to the decorating centre and pick out paint and colours.'

'Can we make new bed things, too?' the child asked, jumping up and down with excitement.

Kirsten laughed at Melissa's enthusiasm. 'Of course.'

'And Joel can help, too. He'd be really good at doing all the tall things.'

Kirsten didn't reply to that, but as Melissa had discovered Jordanne's old music box, complete with ballerina, she need not have worried. How on earth was she going to tell Melissa that Joel probably wouldn't be coming home with them after Christmas?

When they went downstairs, Joel had just arrived home. He was smiling brightly, and as she descended the stairs Kirsten felt her knees begin to wobble. She shook her head, disgusted with her lack of self-control. She watched as he embraced Melissa, smothering the little girl with kisses and tickling her tummy at the same time.

'You're next,' he said, catching sight of her on the stairs. He released Melissa and took the remaining stairs two at a time. 'Hello, there.' He swept her off her feet, planting a big kiss on her lips.

'Careful. Well, you're certainly in a good mood,' she said, her plummeting heart hitting rock bottom. From his attitude, it was obvious he'd been accepted onto the team.

'You'd better believe it.' He looked into her face, his smile fading instantly. 'What's wrong?' He put her down.

Kirsten was unable to hold back the tears that were gathering in the corners of her eyes. 'It's noth...' She stopped and took a deep breath. 'It's time, Joel. I...I need to talk to you.'

'Sure,' he said, his gaze radiating concern. 'Sure.' He led her down the stairs and into the library. 'What's wrong?' he asked again the instant the door was closed.

Kirsten took a few steps away from him towards the mantelpiece. The fireplace had been cleaned after the winter and was now devoid of all logs and paper. She looked up at the family portrait, which had been taken some years ago, and sighed. 'Joel,' she said softly, and turned to face him. 'We need to talk—about us.'

'I see,' he said carefully. 'What exactly is the problem?'

'You,' she said, gesturing to him before running her hand through her hair. She'd specifically left it down, knowing how much he liked it that way, so that when he saw her at the airport he would be pleased.

'I...don't see.'

'Where do you see our relationship heading?' she asked, and a dawning realisation crossed his face. 'I mean, you're going off to the Olympics and you'll be gone for at least four to six months. What happens to us? Am I supposed to wait for you to return? *Will* you return? Do you want to be a permanent partner in my medical practice? Do you want an instant family?'

'Whoa,' he said, and held up his hands. 'This has been brewing for a while, hasn't it,' he asked rhetorically as he took a few steps towards her then stopped before he got too close.

'Yes. I didn't want to put a dampener on your training regime. I know how much the Olympics means to you and I understand, but if I just knew how you felt...' She trailed off and turned away, holding on to the mantelpiece with both hands.

'Do you have any idea how terrible the other week was without you? It was awful.' Her voice was low, filled with remembered anguish. 'Melissa was sick and I was sick and it was just terrible. I have so much sympathy and respect

for single parents now, but I'll tell you something Joel...'
She turned to face him. 'I don't *want* to be a single parent.
I don't *want* to have to cope alone.

'Melissa was beside herself with worry and fear, wondering whether she'd ever see you again. She even asked
me last night again after we'd seen your plane take off. She
loves you so much, Joel, and she depends on you.'

'I know,' he replied, raking his hand through his hair. 'I
know.'

'I love you,' she whispered, her gaze reflecting her
words.

'Oh, honey,' he said, and covered the remaining distance
between them, placing his hands on her shoulders. 'Honey,'
he whispered, lowering his head and pressing his lips firmly
against her own.

There was such promise in the kiss but Kirsten wanted
the romance *and* the words—the three little words that
would tie up all the loose ends of her life. Instead, Joel
reluctantly let her go as the door to the library opened and
Melissa walked in.

'There you are,' she said as she wrapped her hands
around Joel's leg. 'I was looking for you. Jane said you
have to go to the shops before they shut and she said that
if it was all right with Aunty Kirsten, I could go, too.'
Melissa turned her pleading blue gaze up to meet Kirsten's.
'*Please*, Aunty Kirsten. *Please*, can I go to the shops with
Joel? *Please?*'

Kirsten didn't know what to think or say. Her emotions
were strung so taut she wasn't sure what to do.

'We won't be too long,' Joel said as he took Melissa's
hand in his.

'Sure,' Kirsten replied, and nodded.

'Yay! Thanks, Aunty Kirsten,' Melissa said, and gave
her aunt's legs a squeeze before running from the room.

Joel kissed her briefly again before indicating the door.
'I'd better not—'

'Keep her waiting,' Kirsten finished. 'Go.'

'I'll be back soon. We'll work everything out,' he told
her, before following Melissa.

Kirsten sat down in one of the comfortable chairs and
for the first time in weeks found herself unable to cry.
Instead, even though the discussion hadn't gone *quite* as
she'd planned, she felt a weight lifted from her heart just
by having told Joel that she loved him.

How long she sat there for she had no idea, but realised
she must have dozed off when she felt a hand gently shaking her awake.

'Kirsten, dear.'

She recognised the voice of her hostess, Jane McElroy.

'Hmm?'

'Kirsten, wake up.'

She sprang out of the chair, nearly knocking Jane over.
'I'm sorry.' She glanced at the window. It was dark outside.
She smothered a yawn. 'What time is it?'

'It's almost time for dinner. I thought you could use the
snooze,' Jane said kindly, and enveloped Kirsten in a moth-
erly hug. 'Everything's been so busy around here that we
haven't had a proper chance to catch up.' She sat back in
a comfortable chair opposite Kirsten's.

'Are Melissa and Joel back?' Kirsten asked, her eyes
starting to widen in alarm.

'Yes, dear. Melissa is off playing with the other children
and Joel is helping his father set the table.'

'Is there anything I can do to help?'

'Oh, thank you, dear, but everything is running like
clockwork. And thanks to the caterers, even *I'm* not needed
out there at the moment.' She smiled warmly at Kirsten
before saying softly, 'Tell me about you and Joel.'

Kirsten smiled sleepily and sank back into the chair.

'Nothing gets by you, does it? I suppose you've known for years that I liked him.'

Jane simply nodded.

The smile faded and Kirsten closed her eyes. 'I love him, Jane. He's everything to me... yet the Olympics are everything to him.'

'Joel is very similar to his father. When he puts his mind to something, he gives *one hundred per cent* of himself. That's why he's been so successful as a professional athlete. But the other thing I like about Joel is his ability to accept. I think that's one reason he's so good with children. He doesn't push them, or force them to do things. He just sits back and lets them be themselves and then he *accepts* them for who they are. I know both Justin and Jasmine don't have nearly as much patience and acceptance as Joel does, but I guess it's different with your own children.'

They were both silent for a while, listening to the far-off noises around the big, family home. 'I've always believed in miracles, Jane, but lately...' Kirsten trailed off and rubbed her hand wearily across her brow. 'I don't know, perhaps I'm just tired. Too tired to think straight.'

'You're sick of analysing,' Jane supplied, and Kirsten nodded.

'Exactly.'

'Then don't. Stop. Stop analysing everything and just... accept. Accept that Joel is the way he is and, whether he's competing professionally or seeing patients, just keep on loving him for the man he is. If you do that, dear, I can safely promise you that you'll never go wrong.' Jane reached for her hand and gave it a squeeze. 'Now, let's go trim that tree.'

Kirsten felt even better as she quickly went upstairs to change her clothes. She noticed that Melissa had already been changed into her lemon 'wedding' dress as her play clothes were scattered around the floor.

She picked them up and, having dressed in a pair of black trousers and a red and green Christmas top, brushed her hair, added Christmassy earrings and refreshed her make-up. When she descended the stairs again, she felt a lot better.

There were people everywhere. Sally's and Alex's parents had joined the party and, of course, Isobelle and Greg were there, too. Joel's other siblings had their in-laws over too so it really was a 'family' affair.

Everyone was talking as John, Jed and Justin set up the large Christmas tree that would soon be decorated. When it was ready, the festivities began. There were lights and different coloured baubles, tinsel and an assortment of ornaments. Every person there contributed to decorating the tree and as Kirsten closely watched her niece, she saw her wonderment and excitement as the night's events continued to unfold. Melissa played well with Jasmine's and Justin's children and adored Jared's young baby daughter.

Kirsten kept her eye on Joel, who was very happy to be home, rather than on the other side of the world as he'd been last year. She felt a little self-conscious after telling him that she loved him but, still, she was very glad she had. When his gaze met hers across the crowded room, he smiled. A happy, loving smile.

Soon Jane announced it was time for dinner and everyone sat at the long makeshift table that had been set up specifically for the occasion. Kirsten looked at the beautifully inscribed name cards and the amazing Christmas bonbons that Jane had made, just waiting to be pulled. She wondered whether Joel had helped his mother this year, as he'd told her he used to do when he was a child.

John McElroy, as head of the clan, tapped his glass, signalling for silence. He welcomed them all there before asking everyone to bow their heads for the Christmas blessing. When he was finished, and after a chorus of 'Amens', he reached for the bon-bon that had his name scrolled in gold ink on the front.

'The next tradition is to break open the bon-bons. Jane and her merry group of elves have been busy all day, putting the finishing touches on them so, please, enjoy.'

There was the sound of snapping and cracking as bon-bons started to burst open around the table. Kirsten turned to Melissa who was seated in between her and Joel.

'Ready to do yours?' she asked.

Melissa looked from her to Joel and shook her head, a large smile covering her little face. 'Let's do *yours* first, Aunty Kirsten,' she said, and pointed to the one with Kirsten's name on.

Kirsten shrugged and picked it up, holding it out to Melissa and Joel. 'Will you help me to snap it open?'

'Of course,' Joel answered as he took Melissa's hand in his and pulled. When it was open, Kirsten's eyes widened in amazement at what fell out. There was a small piece of rolled up paper, but around it wasn't a piece of ribbon but a diamond ring.

Kirsten gasped in shock and a few people down their end of the table turned to see what was wrong. With trembling hands, she picked it up. She glanced at Joel who was smiling hesitantly at her, unsure of what her reaction might be.

'Read the note, Aunty Kirsten,' Melissa prompted.

Kirsten couldn't move her hands. They were frozen holding the paper and the ring. By now they had everyone's attention, but Kirsten was oblivious to everything but the two people beside her.

Joel patiently reached over and slid the ring off the paper. He reached for her left hand and slid the ring onto the third finger. 'Read the note,' he said softly and this time Kirsten commanded her fingers to work.

As she unrolled it, she looked at the lovely gold ink with red and green glitter around it.

'I did the glitter,' Melissa said brightly, and although Kirsten loved the glitter, she loved the words even more.

It read, I LOVE YOU. MARRY ME. JOEL.

Kirsten gasped again as she looked at the man whose hand was still tenderly holding hers. 'Well?' he asked, the word barely audible.

'What about the Olympics?' she whispered.

'I'm not going.'

It was the last thing she'd expected him to say.

'Why not?' Her voice was stronger as she frowned at him. 'You were so happy today. You were happy when you got back from seeing the coach.'

'Of course I was happy. I'd finally realised that Olympic gold or any amount of Olympic medals won't make me nearly as happy as I feel when I'm with you. You and Melissa. *You're* my gold medals.'

Kirsten didn't know what to say. She looked down at Melissa, realising she was in on this conspiracy. 'What do you think?'

'My mummy and daddy have gone,' Melissa said matter-of-factly, before looking up at Joel with adoration in her eyes. 'Joel said he'd be my new daddy.'

The tears spilled over and the lump in her throat grew bigger at her niece's words. Then Melissa was looking at her again and Kirsten impatiently wiped her free hand across her face, not caring about her make-up.

'Aunty Kirsten, will you be my new mummy?'

Kirsten's lips trembled in disbelief. These were words she'd longed to hear and she was desperately happy that Melissa's grief was healing. She touched the child tenderly on her cheek. 'Yes,' she whispered with an emphatic nod. She raised her eyes to meet Joel's. 'Yes,' she said firmly to him, then a laugh of joy escaped from her lips.

Applause broke out as Joel leaned over Melissa and captured Kirsten's lips with his own. Then he scooped the little girl up onto his knee and moved onto her chair so they could all embrace together.

'*My* family,' Melissa said with contentment.

EPILOGUE

'SIT *down*, please, Matilda, or you'll spill that drink everywhere,' Kirsten said firmly to her daughter who finally did as she was told. 'I wish I had Joel's patience,' she mumbled to Jordanne and Sally who'd come over for a family barbeque.

'She's two,' Sally said as she picked up Jane, one of Jordanne's twelve-week-old triplets. 'While this little bundle of joy is usually so content, just like her uncles.'

Little Jane was making an awful noise and Jordanne held out her hands for her daughter. 'Give her here. Honestly, I feel like a milking machine some days.'

Kirsten and Sally laughed. 'At least you're not pregnant any more,' Kirsten said, and Jordanne nodded emphatically.

'It's Sally's turn again,' Jordanne said with a smug smile, and Sally patted her rounded stomach.

'Well, Tommy is almost three and he needs a brother or sister to play with,' Sally said with determination.

'Everything under control?' a male voice said from the doorway, and they all turned to look at Alex. He crossed to the special pram to check on Annabelle and Charlotte who were, thankfully, sound asleep. 'It's awful when all three of them are awake at two o'clock in the morning and I have a long surgical list to get through that day.'

'I can imagine,' Kirsten said.

'How's the food coming along?' Sally asked.

'Almost ready,' Jed answered from the doorway as he crossed to his wife's side. 'Hungry?'

'Definitely,' she answered.

He kissed her. 'Where's Tommy?'

'He's watching Melissa play on the computer,' Kirsten answered. 'I guess it's time for them to stop and wash their hands now.'

'I'll get them,' Jed said, and headed off to the study.

'Are we ready to eat?' Joel asked as he came in the door, complete with chef's apron and hat.

Kirsten smiled over at her husband with love shining brightly in her eyes. Matilda had finished her drink and launched herself at her father. Joel scooped her up into his arms and tickled her tummy.

'Let's get this feast under way before the baby starts protesting that I'm not feeding it enough,' Sally said as she headed outside into the sunshine. Kirsten followed suit, and as she stepped out into the garden she was once more stuck by the simple beauty of the bottle-brush trees Joel had planted for her three years ago.

She sighed as Melissa came up and placed her arm around her mother. The seven-year-old looked so much like Jacqui that sometimes Kirsten found it hard to hold back the tears. Although Melissa called her 'Mum', together they both kept the memory of her *real* parents alive.

'All right, McElroy and Page families,' Joel called as everyone trooped outside. 'The food's getting cold so let's eat.'

As the sounds of contented, happy chatter rang out and people helped themselves to the food, Joel crossed to Kirsten's side and nuzzled her neck.

'I love you, Mrs McElroy,' he said.

'The feeling's mutual,' she replied, and pressed her lips firmly to his—where they belonged.

Modern Romance™
...seduction and
passion guaranteed

Tender Romance™
...love affairs that
last a lifetime

Sensual Romance™
...sassy, sexy and
seductive

Blaze™
...sultry days and
steamy nights

Medical Romance™
...medical drama on
the pulse

Historical Romance™
...rich, vivid and
passionate

29 new titles every month.

*With all kinds of Romance for
every kind of mood...*

MILLS & BOON®

Makes any time special™   MAT4

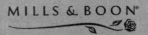

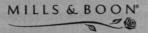

FREE

2 BOOKS
AND A SURPRISE GIFT!

We would like to take this opportunity to thank you for reading this Mills & Boon® book by offering you the chance to take TWO more specially selected titles from the Medical Romance™ series absolutely FREE! We're also making this offer to introduce you to the benefits of the Reader Service™ —

★ FREE home delivery
★ FREE monthly Newsletter
★ FREE gifts and competitions
★ Exclusive Reader Service discount
★ Books available before they're in the shops

Accepting these FREE books and gift places you under no obligation to buy; you may cancel at any time, even after receiving your free shipment. Simply complete your details below and return the entire page to the address below. *You don't even need a stamp!*

YES! Please send me 2 free Medical Romance books and a surprise gift. I understand that unless you hear from me, I will receive 4 superb new titles every month for just £2.49 each, postage and packing free. I am under no obligation to purchase any books and may cancel my subscription at any time. The free books and gift will be mine to keep in any case.

MIZEC

Ms/Mrs/Miss/Mr ....Initials ....
BLOCK CAPITALS PLEASE

Surname ....

Address ....

....

....Postcode ....

Send this whole page to:
UK: FREEPOST CN81, Croydon, CR9 3WZ
EIRE: PO Box 4546, Kilcock, County Kildare (stamp required)